TESTING, TESTING, 1 . . . 2 . . . 3 . . . BATMAN . . .

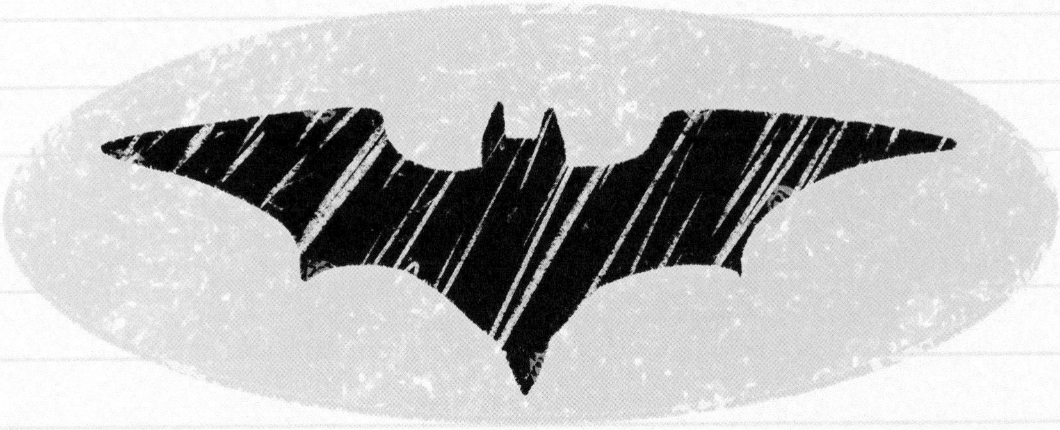

TESTING OUT MY PEN TO SEE IF IT WORKS . . . IT DOES, OH GOOD.

I AM BATMAN!

ACTIVITY BOOK WITH STICKERS

TEXT (THAT'S THE WORDS), ACTIVITIES, DRAWINGS, PLUS AN AWESOME STICKER SECTION IN THE BACK.

BY

BATMAN
(THAT'S ME!)

LEGO

THE LEGO BATMAN MOVIE

I'M BATMAN!™

THE DARK KNIGHT'S ACTIVITY BOOK WITH STICKERS

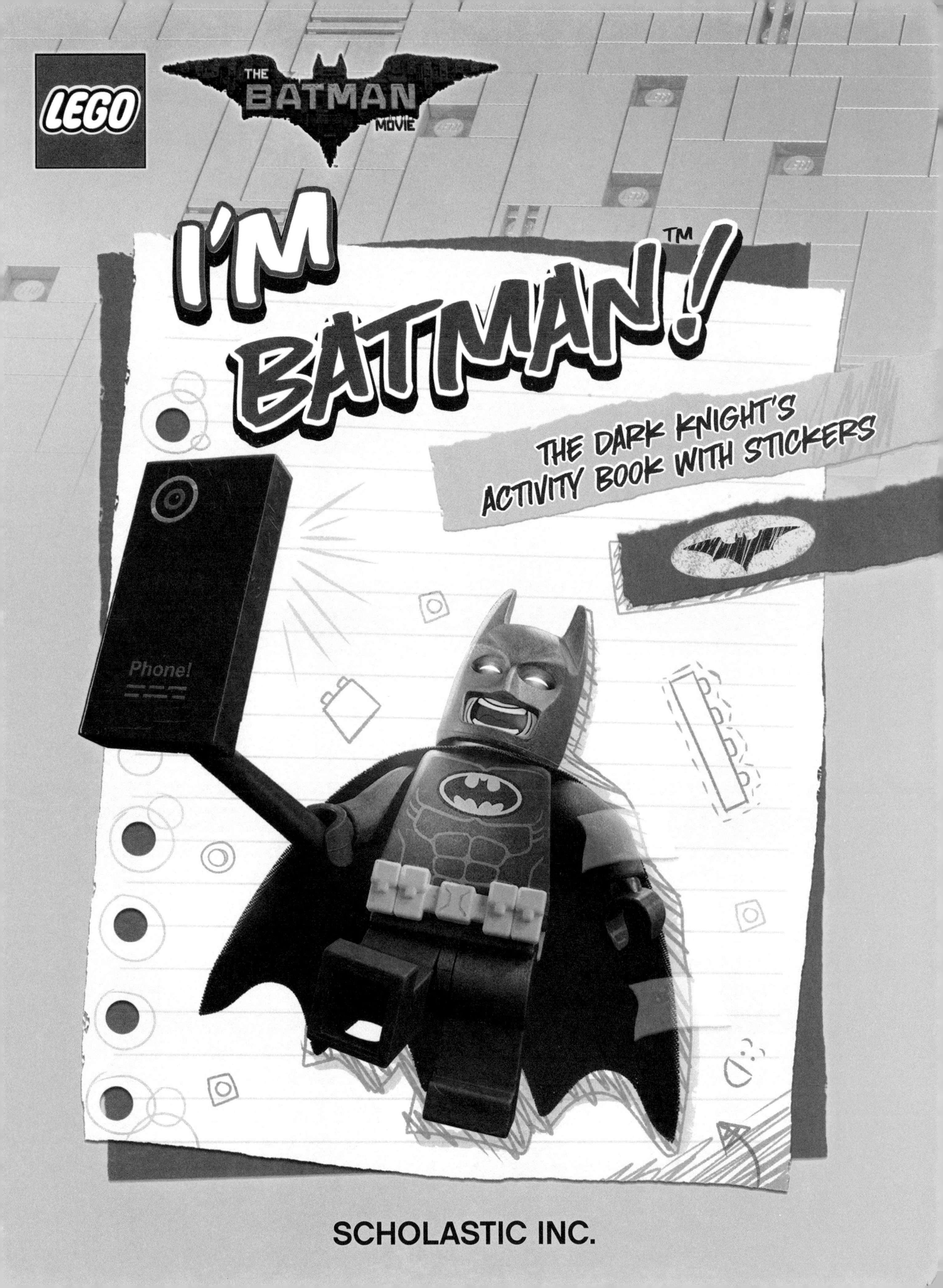
Phone!

SCHOLASTIC INC.

Based on the screenplay by Seth Grahame-Smith and Chris McKenna & Erik Sommers,
with additional material by Jared Stern & John Whittington, based on LEGO Construction Toys.

All rights reserved. Published by Scholastic Inc., *Publishers since 1920.* SCHOLASTIC
and associated logos are trademarks and/or registered trademarks of Scholastic Inc.

ISBN 978-1-338-11223-8

10 9 8 7 6 5 4 3 2 1   17 18 19 20 21

Printed in the U.S.A.   40
First printing 2017

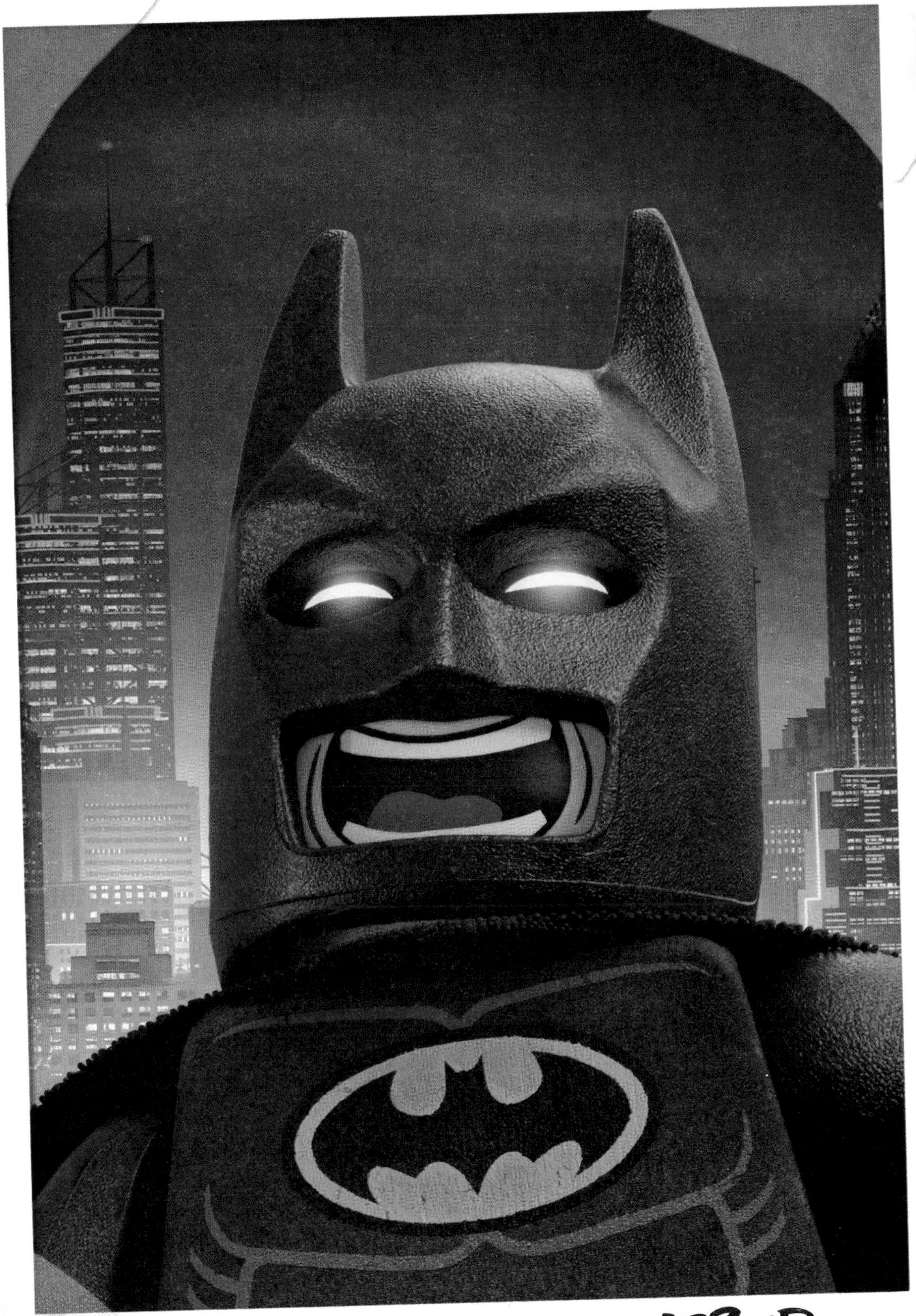

AREN'T I HANDSOME? :D

I AM BATMAN.

AND I'VE DECIDED TO START A JOURNAL FOR MY GREATEST FANS! BECAUSE I DON'T JUST HAVE FANS . . .

I HAVE THE **GREATEST FANS!** BECAUSE **I'M BATMAN** AND YOU, MY FANS, ARE AMAZING.

SO, THIS IS WHAT I WANTED TO WRITE . . .

HMM . . . THIS "WRITING A JOURNAL" LARK ISN'T ALL THAT EASY.

PORTRAIT OF TEMPORARY WRITER'S BLOCK.

MAYBE IT'S BEST TO START WITH A PICTURE OF ONE OF
MY GREATEST FANS.

DRAW A PICTURE OR STICK A PHOTO OF YOURSELF HERE,
WHILE I GATHER MY THOUGHTS.

OK, IT'S TIME TO HAVE SOME FUN. LET'S START WITH
THE COOLEST INTRODUCTION TO A BOOK EVER . . .

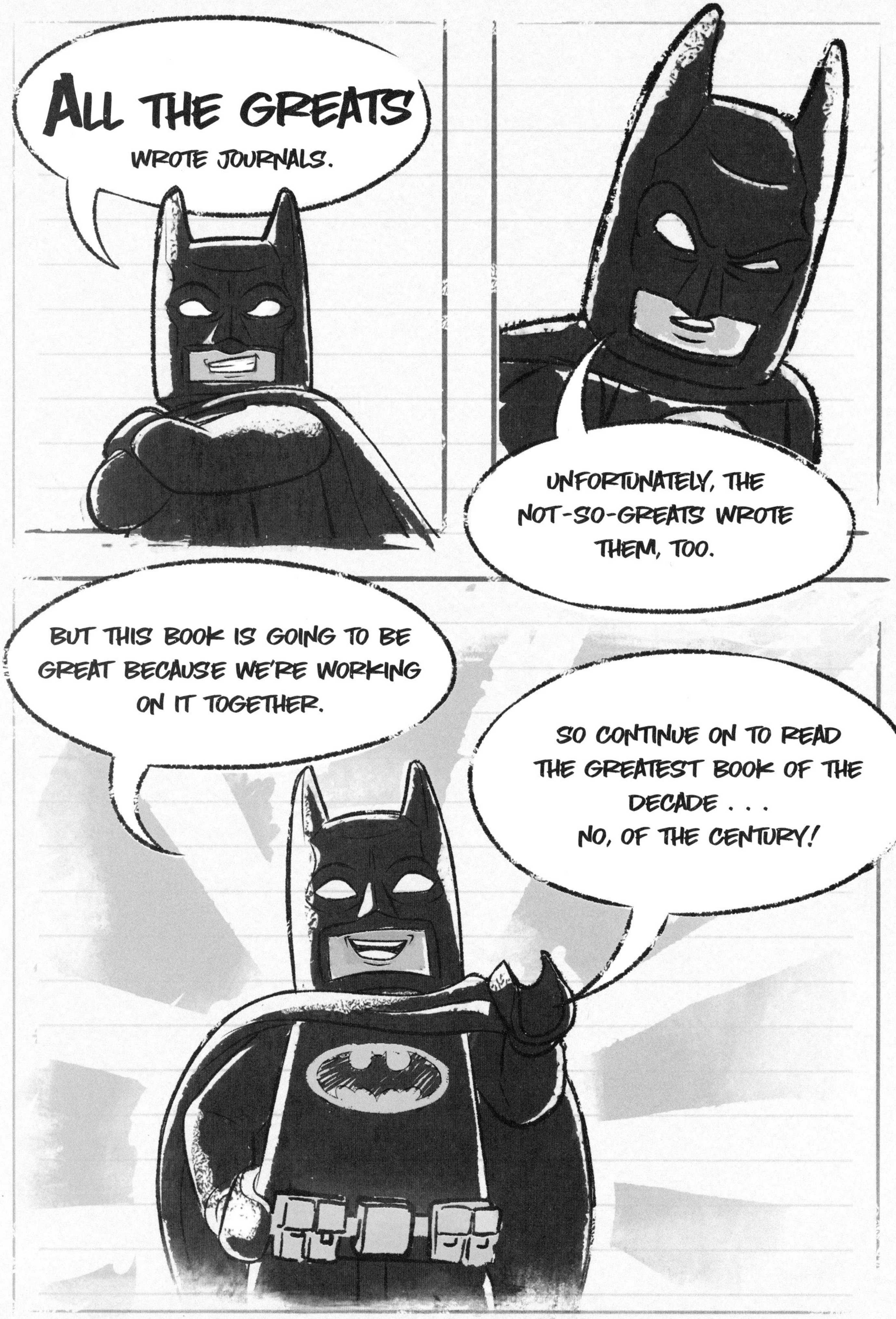
ALL THE GREATS WROTE JOURNALS.
UNFORTUNATELY, THE NOT-SO-GREATS WROTE THEM, TOO.
BUT THIS BOOK IS GOING TO BE GREAT BECAUSE WE'RE WORKING ON IT TOGETHER.
SO CONTINUE ON TO READ THE GREATEST BOOK OF THE DECADE . . . NO, OF THE CENTURY!

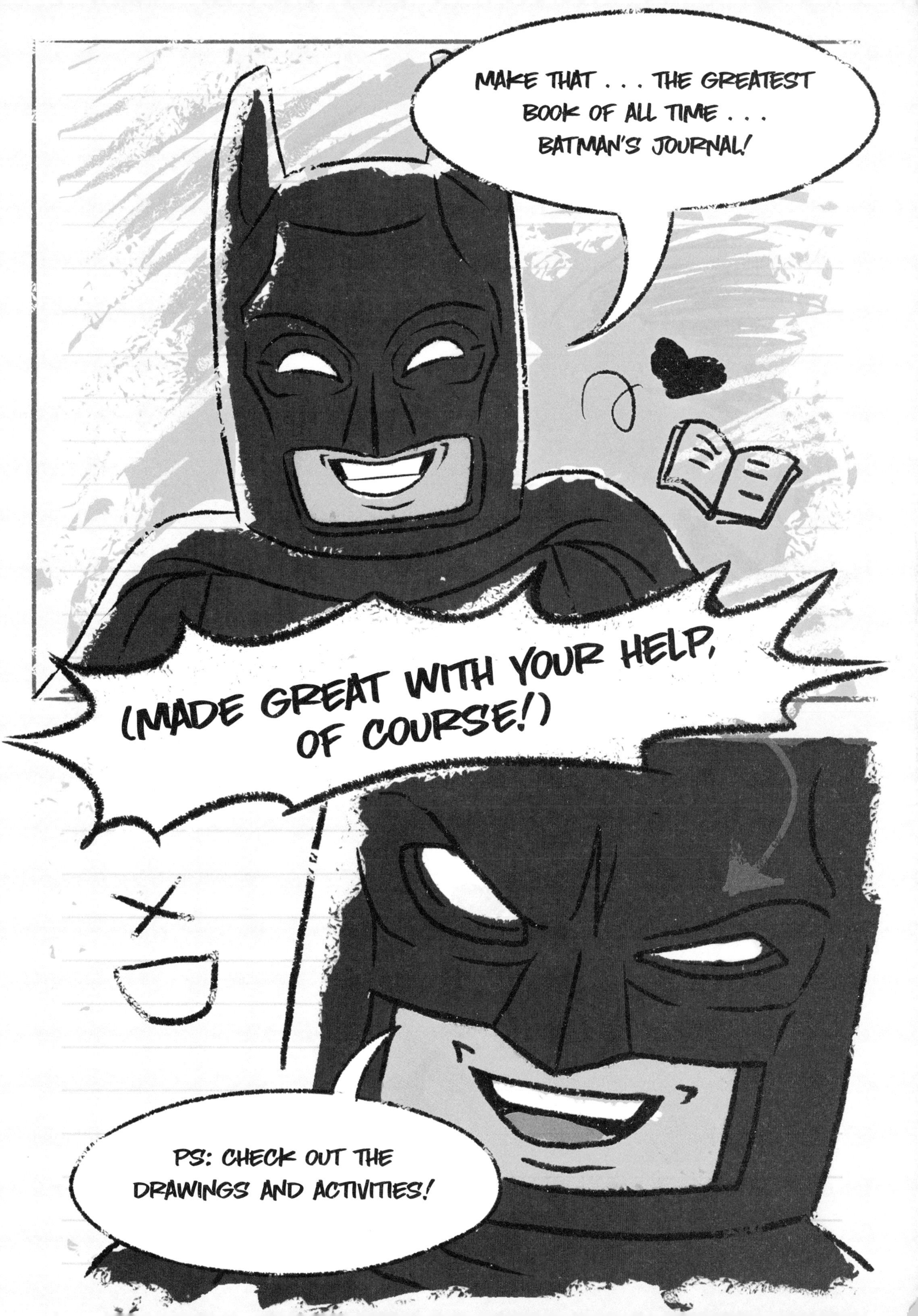
MAKE THAT . . . THE GREATEST BOOK OF ALL TIME . . . BATMAN'S JOURNAL!
(MADE GREAT WITH YOUR HELP, OF COURSE!)
PS: CHECK OUT THE DRAWINGS AND ACTIVITIES!

I'M A SUPER HERO.

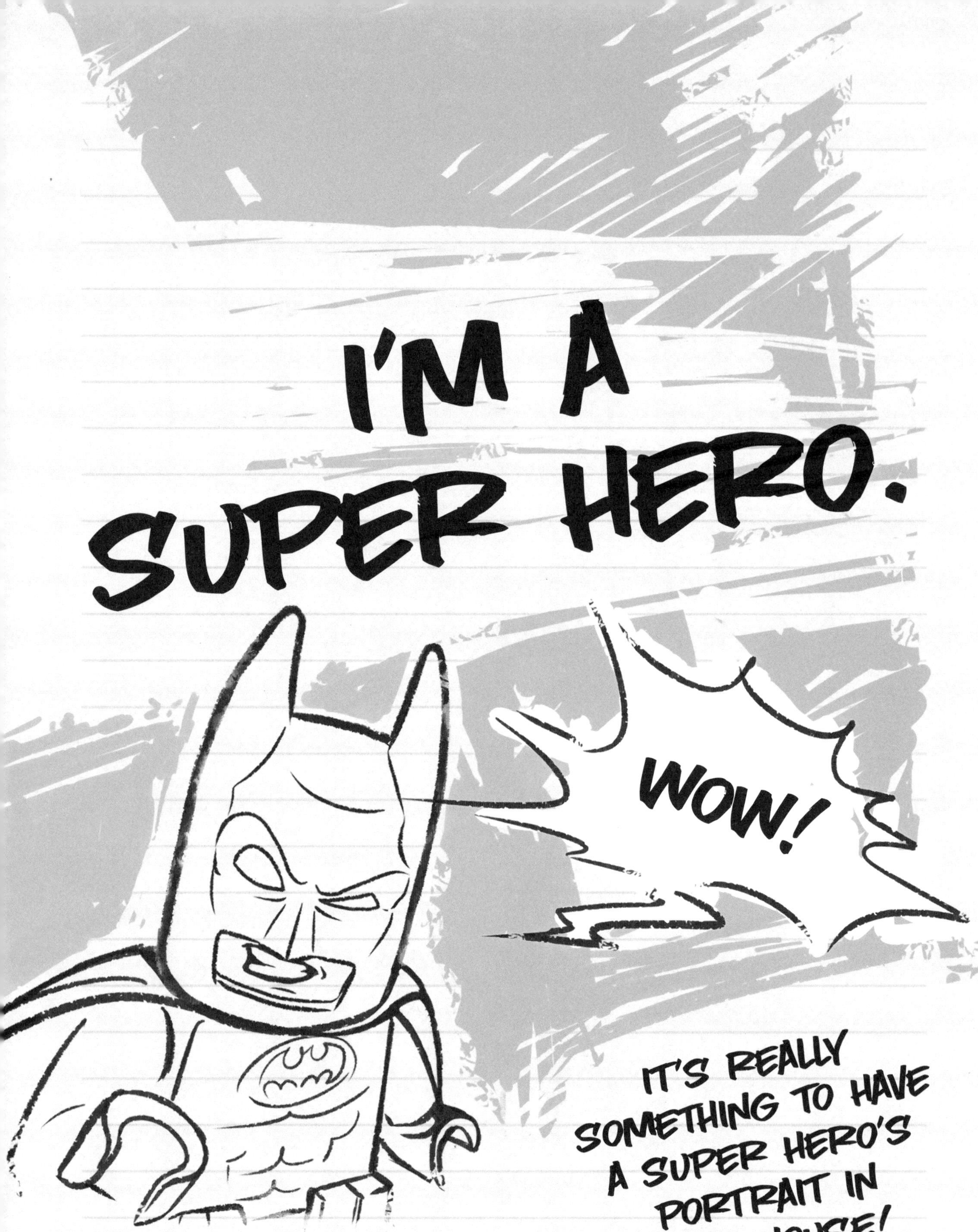
WOW!

IT'S REALLY SOMETHING TO HAVE A SUPER HERO'S PORTRAIT IN YOUR HOUSE!

HERE'S HOW TO DRAW MY PORTRAIT IN THREE SIMPLE STEPS:

STEP 1

DRAW THE SHAPE OF MY HEAD AND SHOULDERS.

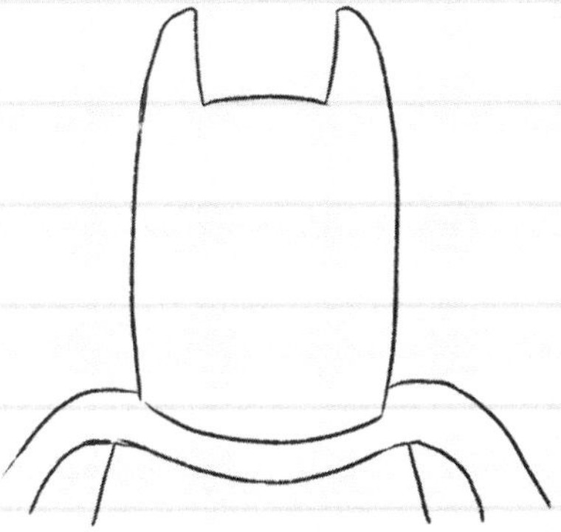

STEP 2

DRAW MY MASK AND EYES.

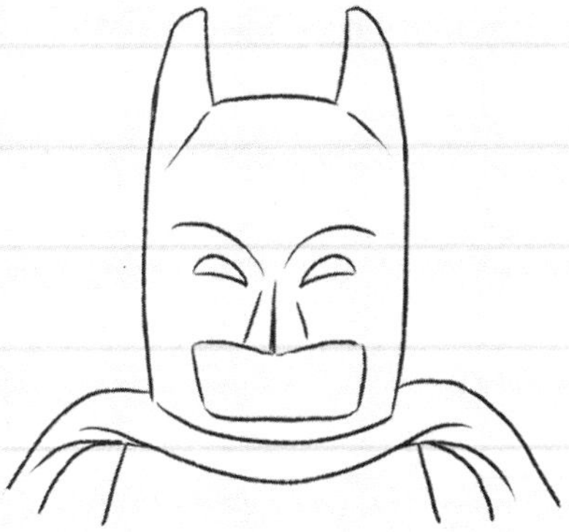

STEP 3

AND THEN DRAW THE REST OF ME LIKE THIS! HERE IT IS – PERFECTION.

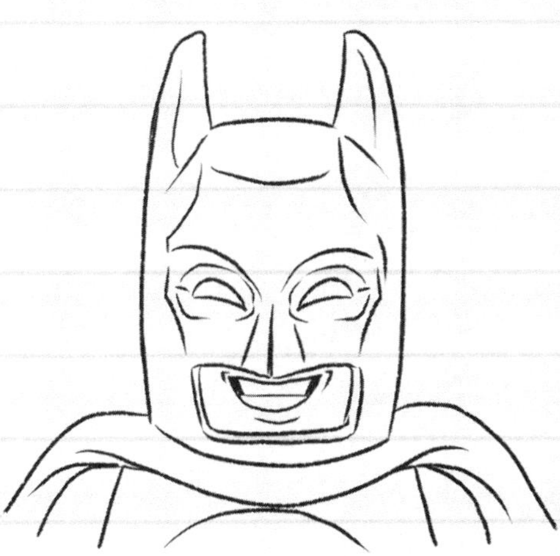

(ROUND OF

APPLAUSE

PLEASE!)

DRAW A PICTURE OF YOURSELF DRESSED AS BATMAN HERE.

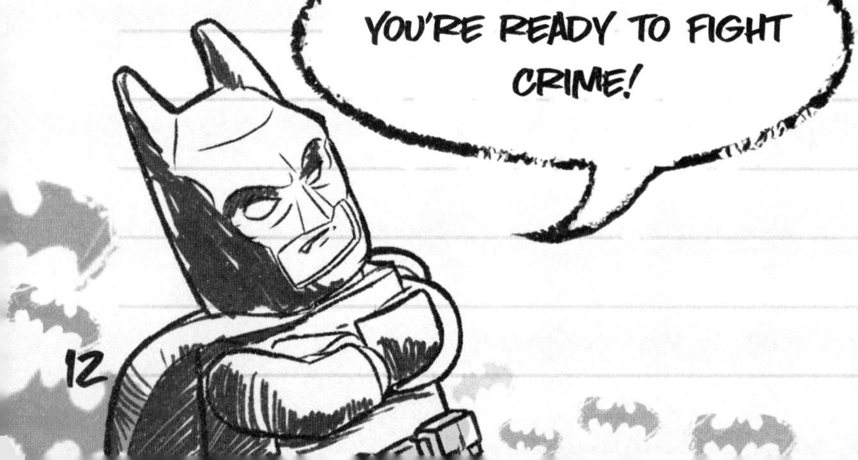
YOU'RE READY TO FIGHT CRIME!

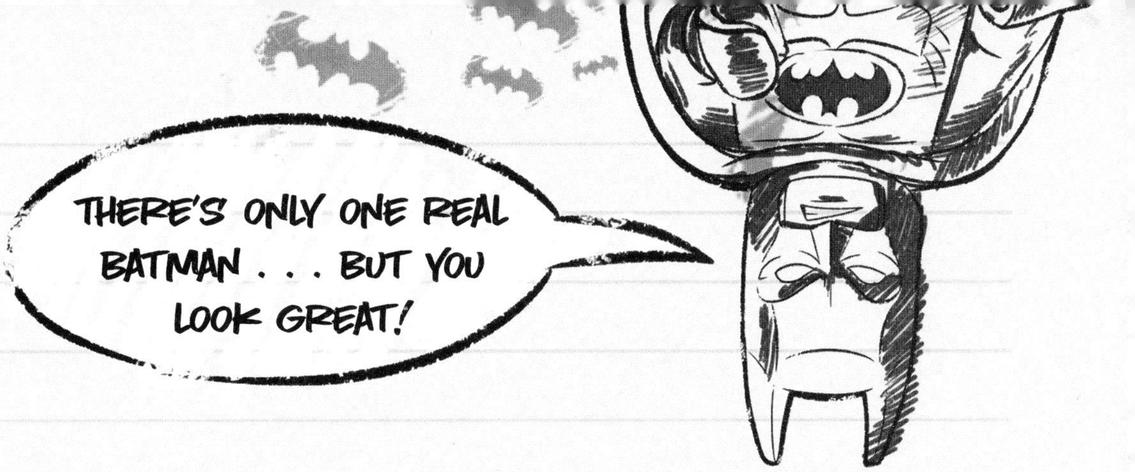
THERE'S ONLY ONE REAL BATMAN . . . BUT YOU LOOK GREAT!

DRAW A COOL VEHICLE FOR YOURSELF HERE, TOO!

HAS ANYTHING EXCITING HAPPENED TODAY?
WELL, I SAVED THE CITY AGAIN.
THE NIGHT PATROL WAS AWESOME!

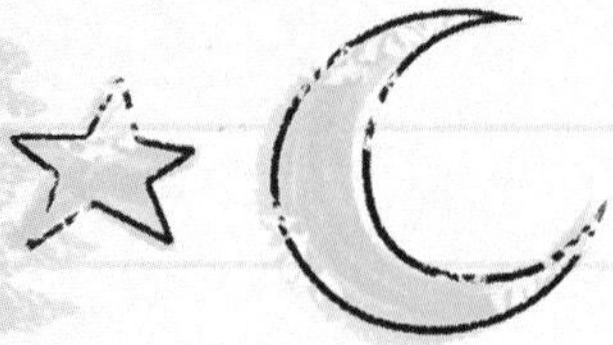

FIRST, **JEWELS** WERE STOLEN FROM THE MUSEUM!

BUT I DID MY SHADOW TRICK . . .
THIS IS THE ONE WHERE I SUDDENLY
EMERGE FROM THE DARKNESS,
WAVING MY CAPE, AND MY SHADOW
LOOKS LIKE A GIANT BAT.

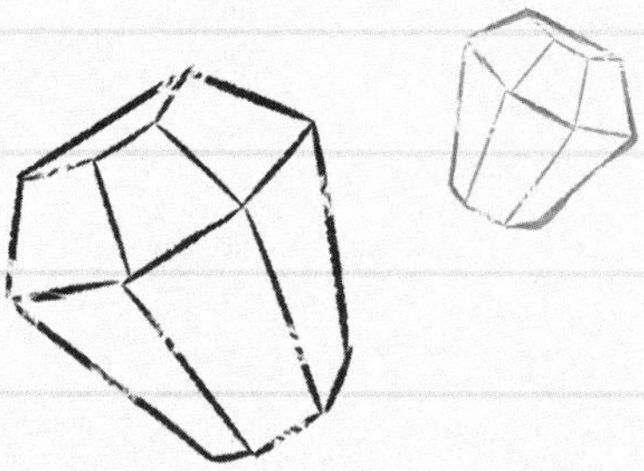

SOMETIMES I REALLY ENJOY
WATCHING VILLAINS GET

SCARED!

THEN, THERE WAS A BANK ROBBERY.
THEY REALLY SHOULD KNOW BETTER THAN TO TRY A
BREAK-IN WHEN I'M PROTECTING THE CITY.
AND IN THE MORNING I HAD TO DEAL WITH A STREET GANG
OF BRICK THIEVES . . .

I'M SO FAST THAT

SOMETIMES

I AMAZE MYSELF!

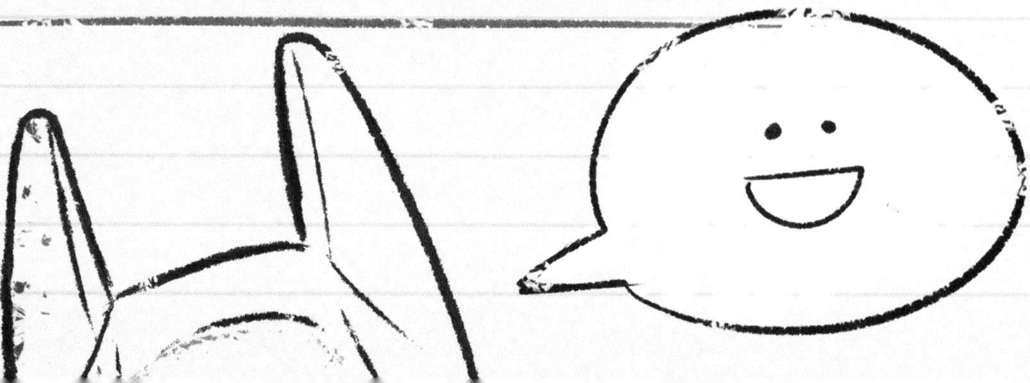

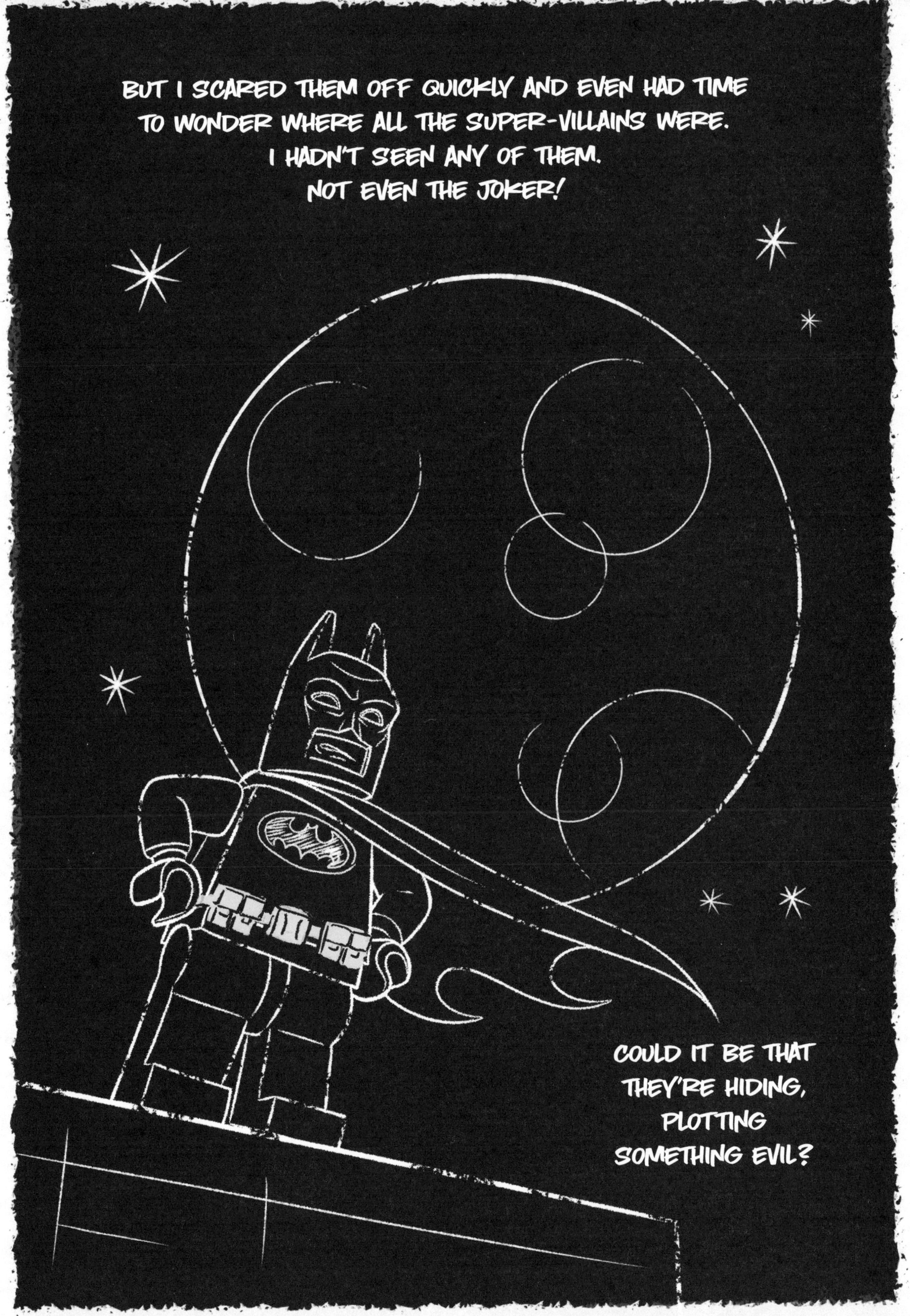
BUT I SCARED THEM OFF QUICKLY AND EVEN HAD TIME TO WONDER WHERE ALL THE SUPER-VILLAINS WERE. I HADN'T SEEN ANY OF THEM. NOT EVEN THE JOKER!
COULD IT BE THAT THEY'RE HIDING, PLOTTING SOMETHING EVIL?

TIME FOR ME TO TELL YOU AN INTERESTING FACT: EVERY SUPER HERO HAS AN

ARCH-NEMESIS!

A NEMESIS IS AN OPPONENT WHO CAN SOMETIMES MAKE YOU REALLY ANGRY. ESPECIALLY SOMEONE LIKE THE JOKER — PICTURED BELOW.

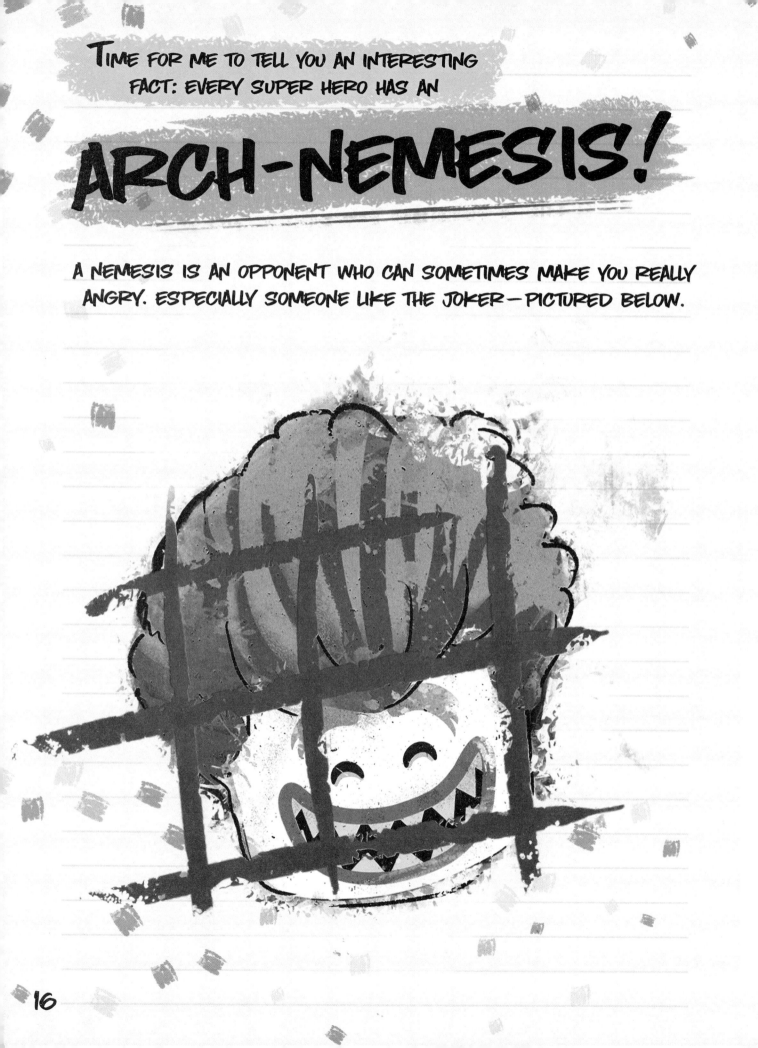

USE YOUR IMAGINATION TO DRAW ME ANOTHER CHALLENGING OPPONENT AND GIVE THEM A NAME THAT'S FIT FOR A SUPER-VILLAIN!

WHAT SUPERPOWERS DO THEY HAVE?

OK, MY GREATEST FANS!
I'D LIKE TO SHOW YOU MY SECRET HQ. IT'S CALLED THE BATCAVE AND IT'S THE BIGGEST HEADQUARTERS THE WORLD HAS EVER SEEN! IT IS LOCATED UNDERNEATH MY—BRUCE WAYNE'S—MANSION.
BUT THAT'S
TOP SECRET!
I BET YOU'RE WONDERING WHAT MY HEADQUARTERS LOOK LIKE, BUT THAT'S TOP SECRET, TOO. DESIGN WHAT YOU THINK THE BATCAVE LOOKS LIKE HERE.

SECRET HQ

AND NOW SOME FACTS ABOUT ME:

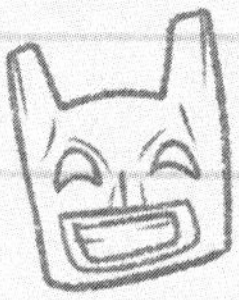

I KNOW OVER **127** MARTIAL ART STYLES. (TAKE THAT!)

THEY CALL ME THE **WORLD'S GREATEST DETECTIVE**. (AND THEY'RE PROBABLY RIGHT!)

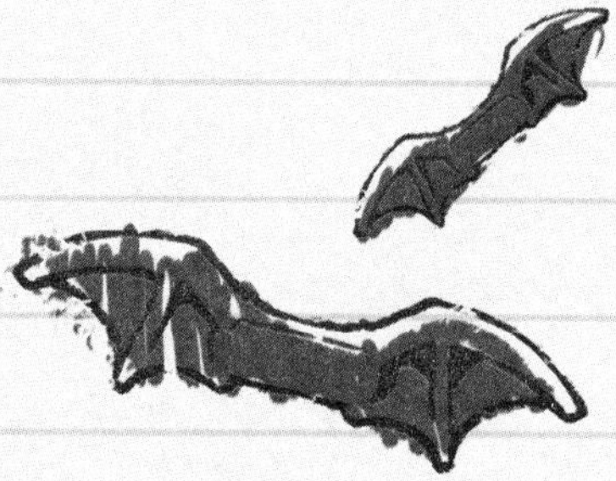

MANY SAY I AM UNBELIEVABLY
SMART AND WITTY.
(AND I THANK THEM VERY MUCH FOR IT.)

MAN! THIS KICK IS REALLY AWESOME!

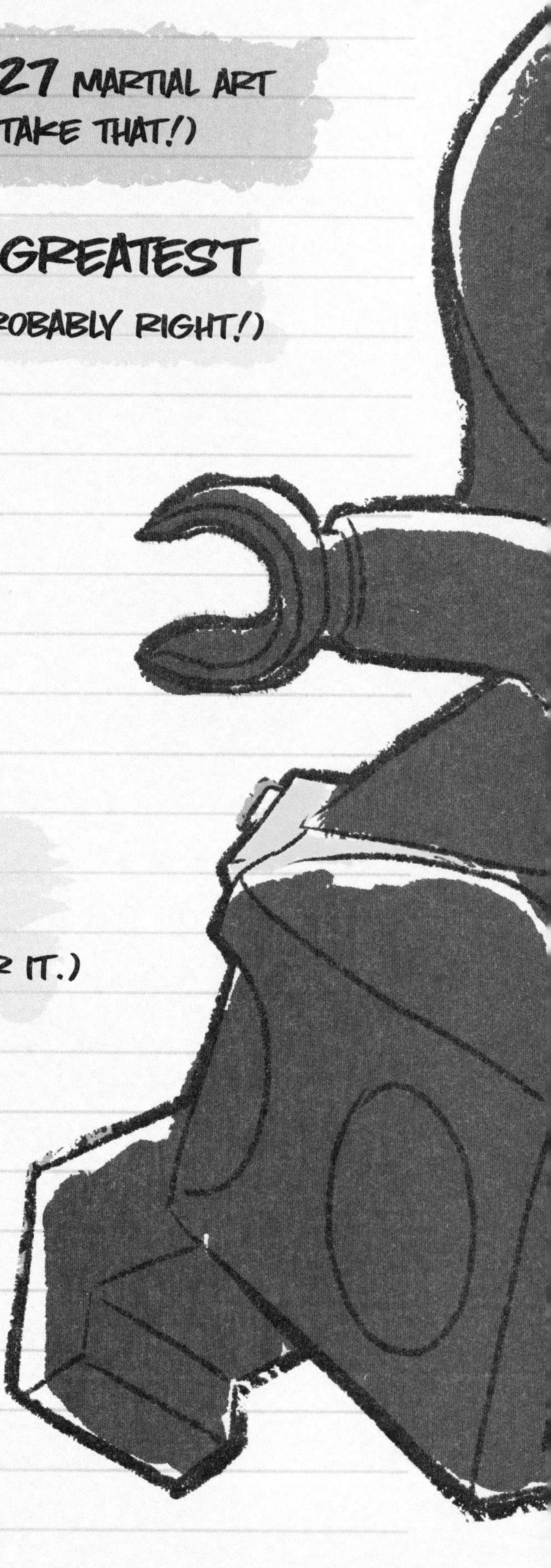

MY COSTUME IS REALLY IMPRESSIVE. (WELL, THEY DO SAY "DRESS TO IMPRESS"!)

MY VEHICLES ARE SO COOL. (IT'S ALWAYS BEST TO TRAVEL IN STYLE!)

MY FRIEND AND LOYAL BUTLER'S NAME IS ALBERT PENNYWORTH. (I LOVE HIM!)

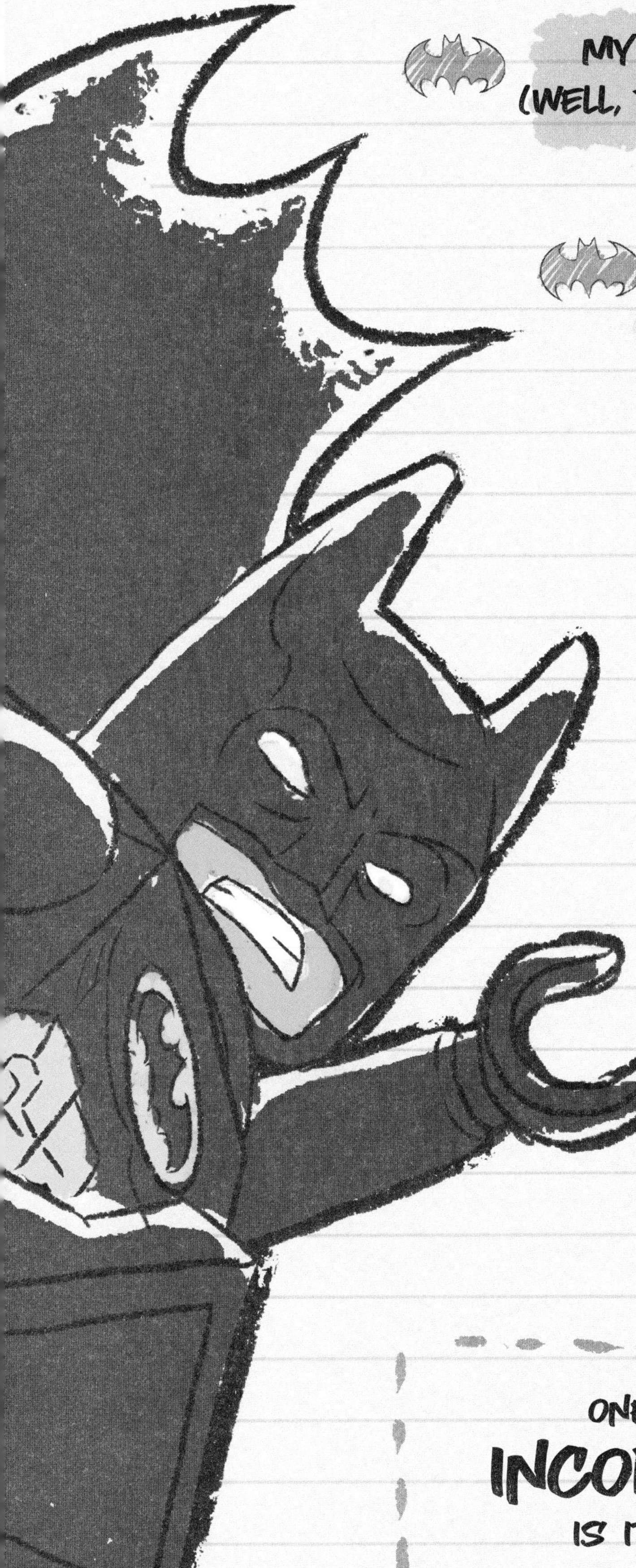

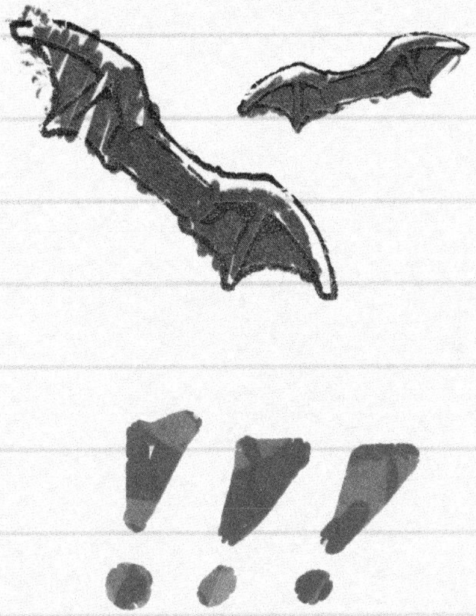

ONE OF THESE FUN FACTS IS **INCORRECT!** BUT WHICH ONE IS IT? LOOK FOR THE ANSWER IN THIS BOOK. :)

HAS ANYTHING EXCITING HAPPENED TODAY?

WELL, I SAVED THE CITY AGAIN!

MY OPPONENTS CALL THEMSELVES

THE ROGUES.

AND I'M SURE I DON'T NEED TO REMIND YOU WHO GATHERED THEM ALL TOGETHER!

THEY TRIED TO TAKE CONTROL OF GOTHAM'S ENERGY FACILITY AND THAT WAS **A BIG MISTAKE!**

DON'T WORRY, I SOON MADE THEM REALIZE THEIR

MISTAKE!

HEE HEE HEE!

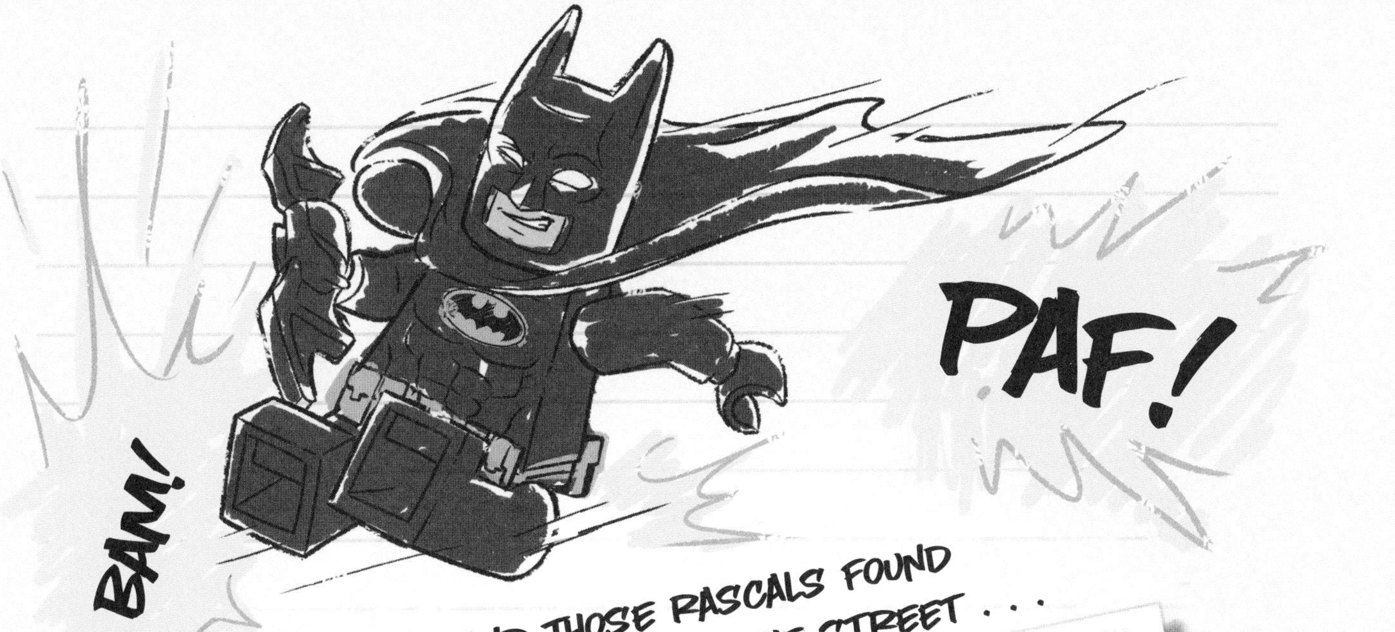
PAF!
BAM!

WHAM! AND THOSE RASCALS FOUND
THEMSELVES FACEDOWN IN THE STREET . . .

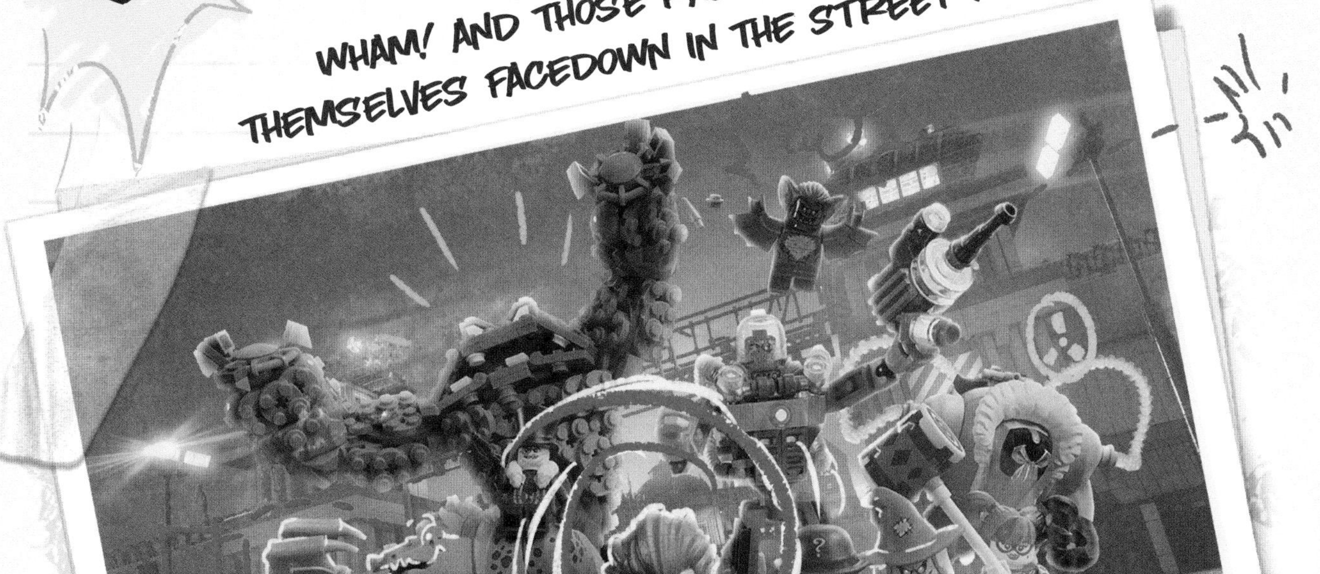

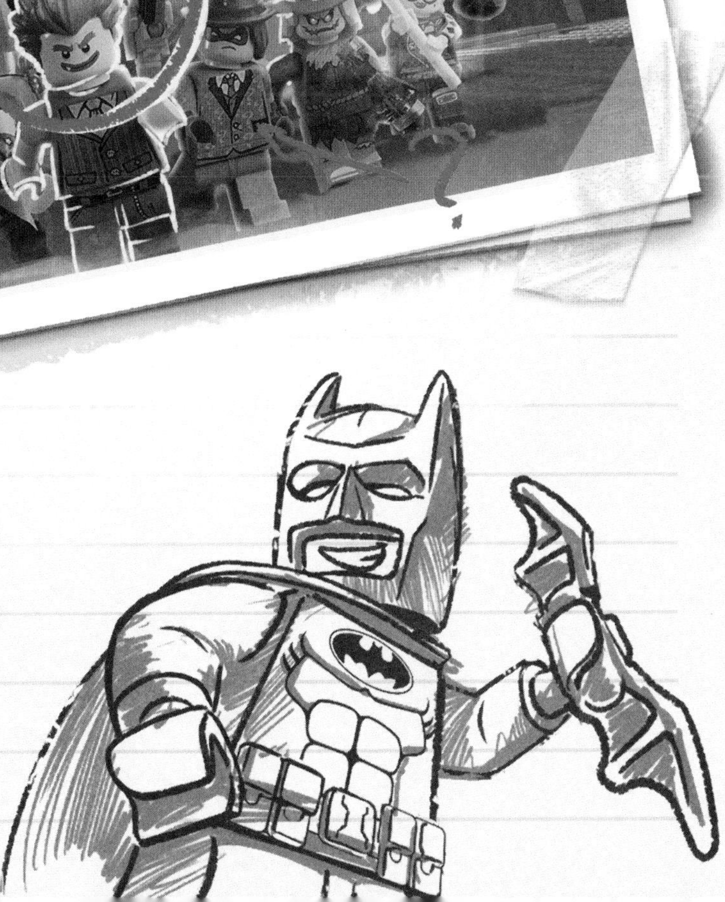

DESIGN SOME NEW GADGETS FOR ME.

REMEMBER TO USE
THE BAT-SYMBOL
IN YOUR DRAWINGS . . .

I'D LOVE A JET BACKPACK, TOO, WHILE YOU'RE AT IT!

. . . AND INVENT SOME **AWESOME** NAMES FOR THEM!

ALFRED TAKES CARE OF ALL MY GADGETS AND KEEPS EVERYTHING IN ORDER.

25

I'M NOT SURE

IF I'VE FORMALLY INTRODUCED

ALFRED

TO YOU.

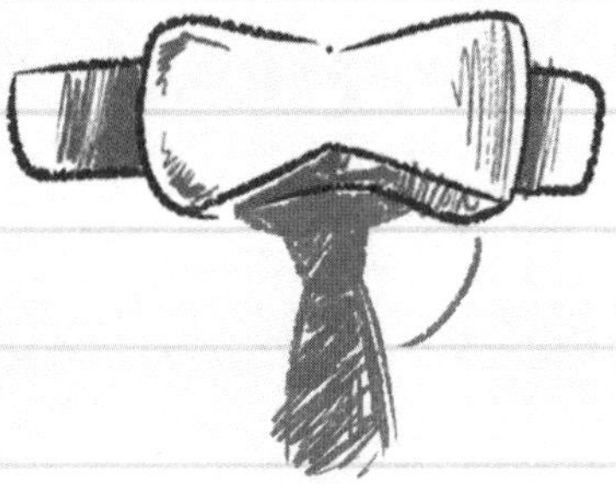

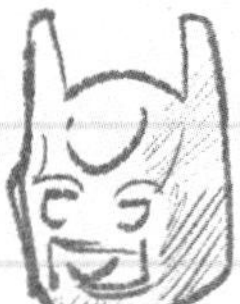

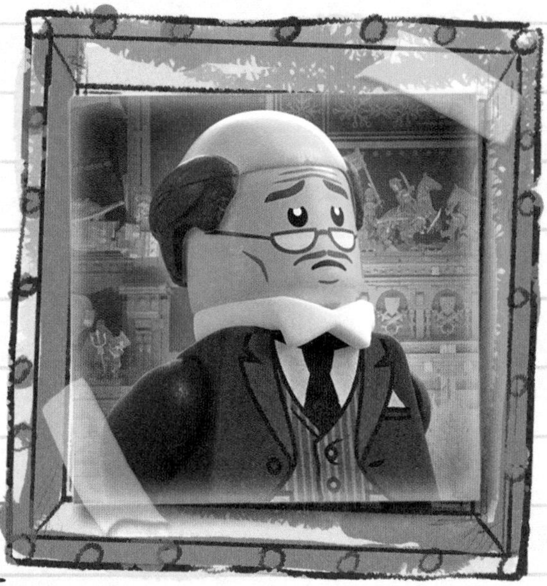

HE'S MY **FRIEND** AND ASSISTANT, AND HE USED TO BE AN **ACTOR!**

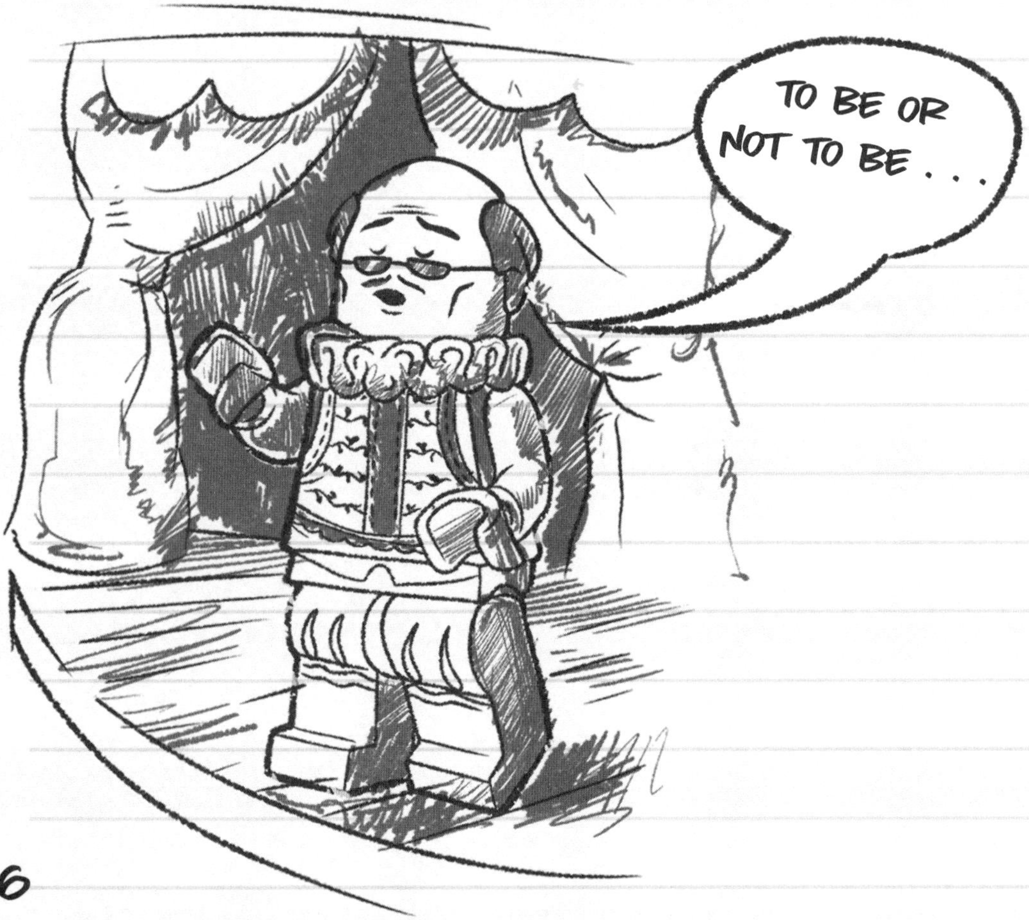
TO BE OR NOT TO BE . . .

DRAW **ALFRED** STARRING IN AN **AMAZING MOVIE** RIGHT HERE ON THIS PAGE!

ANSWER TO PAGE 21:
MY FRIEND AND BUTLER IS NAMED ALFRED NOT ALBERT. :)

GOTHAM CITY . . . MY CITY. THE STREETS ARE AS FULL OF VILLAINS AS THE CAVES ARE OF BATS. SOMETIMES THEY ARE SUPER-VILLAINS, TOO . . . I DON'T CARE WHAT THEY ARE. WHEN THEY MEET ME, THEY'RE **DOOMED!**

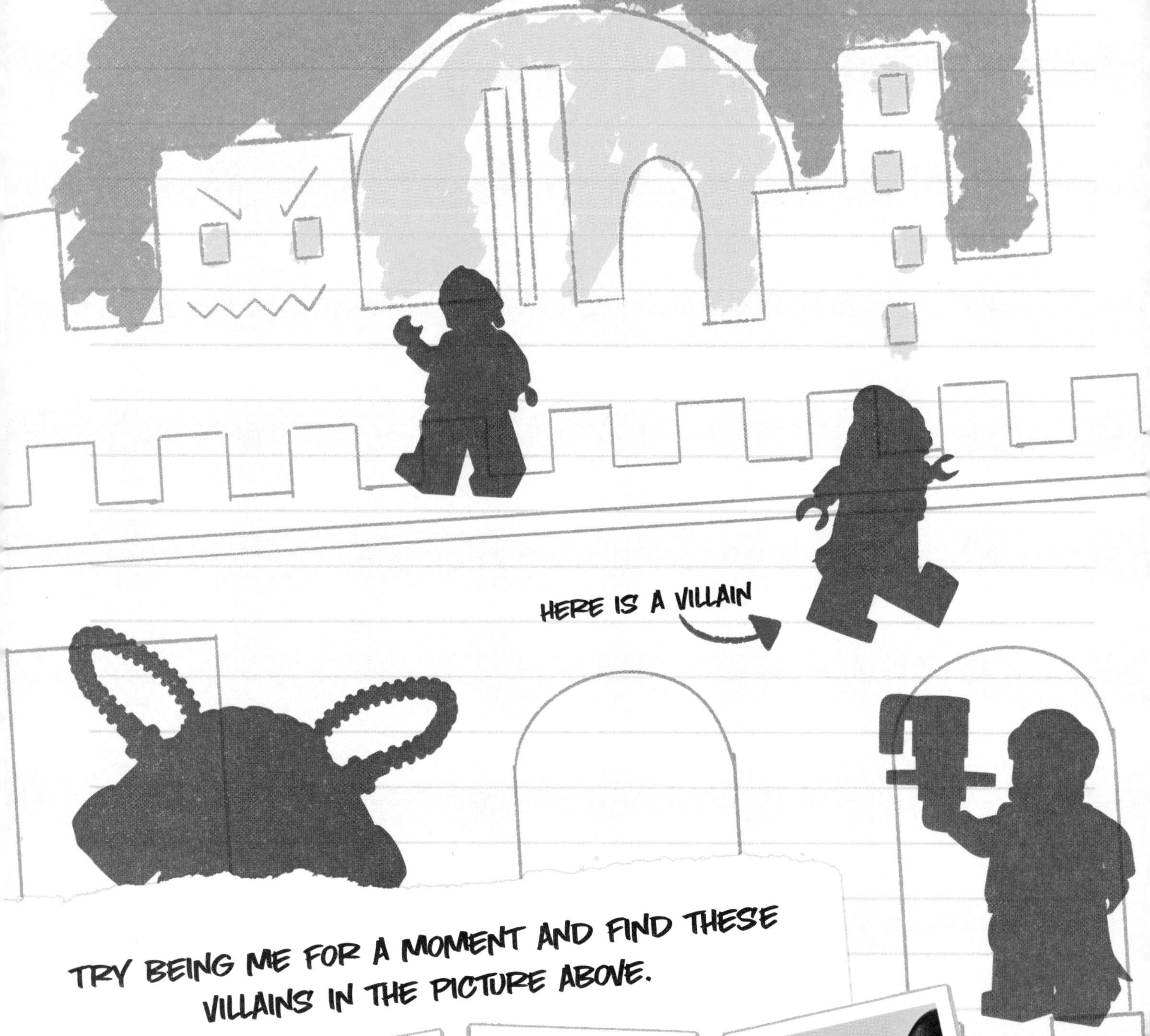
HERE IS A VILLAIN

TRY BEING ME FOR A MOMENT AND FIND THESE VILLAINS IN THE PICTURE ABOVE.

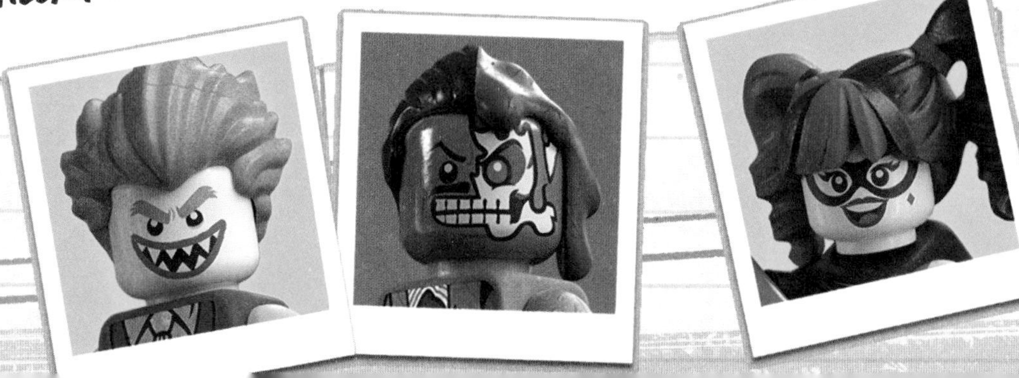

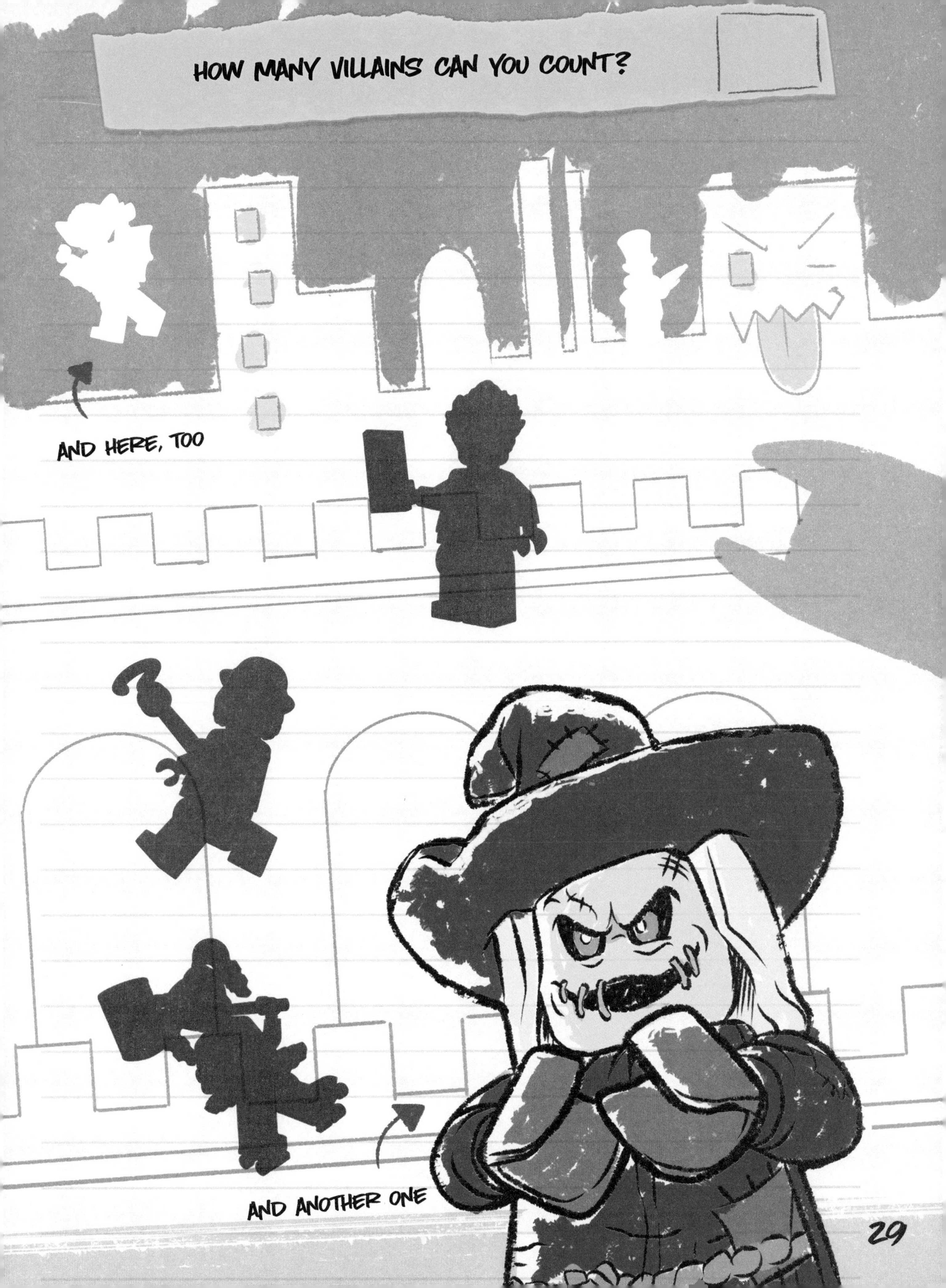
HOW MANY VILLAINS CAN YOU COUNT?
AND HERE, TOO
AND ANOTHER ONE

AS A SUPER HERO

I HAVE SOME PRETTY **AWESOME LINES** TO SAY TO SUPER-VILLAINS.

IN MY SPARE TIME I LIKE TO JOT DOWN COOL LINES TO USE IN THE FUTURE. HERE ARE SOME EXAMPLES:

CAN YOU SEE MY FACE? IT'S THE FACE OF JUSTICE!

(WARNING! NEVER USE THIS LINE IN A DARK ALLEY)

YOU THINK YOU KNOW NO FEAR? I'M YOUR BIGGEST FEAR!

(WARNING! USE ONLY IN DARK ALLEYS)

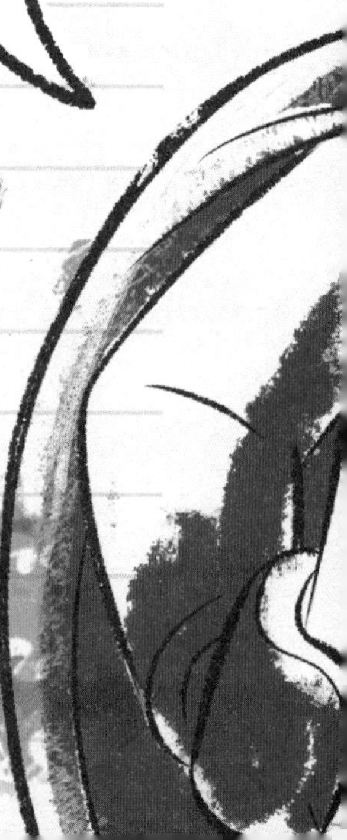

WHAT GREAT LINES CAN YOU COME UP WITH? WRITE THEM IN THE EMPTY SPEECH BUBBLES.

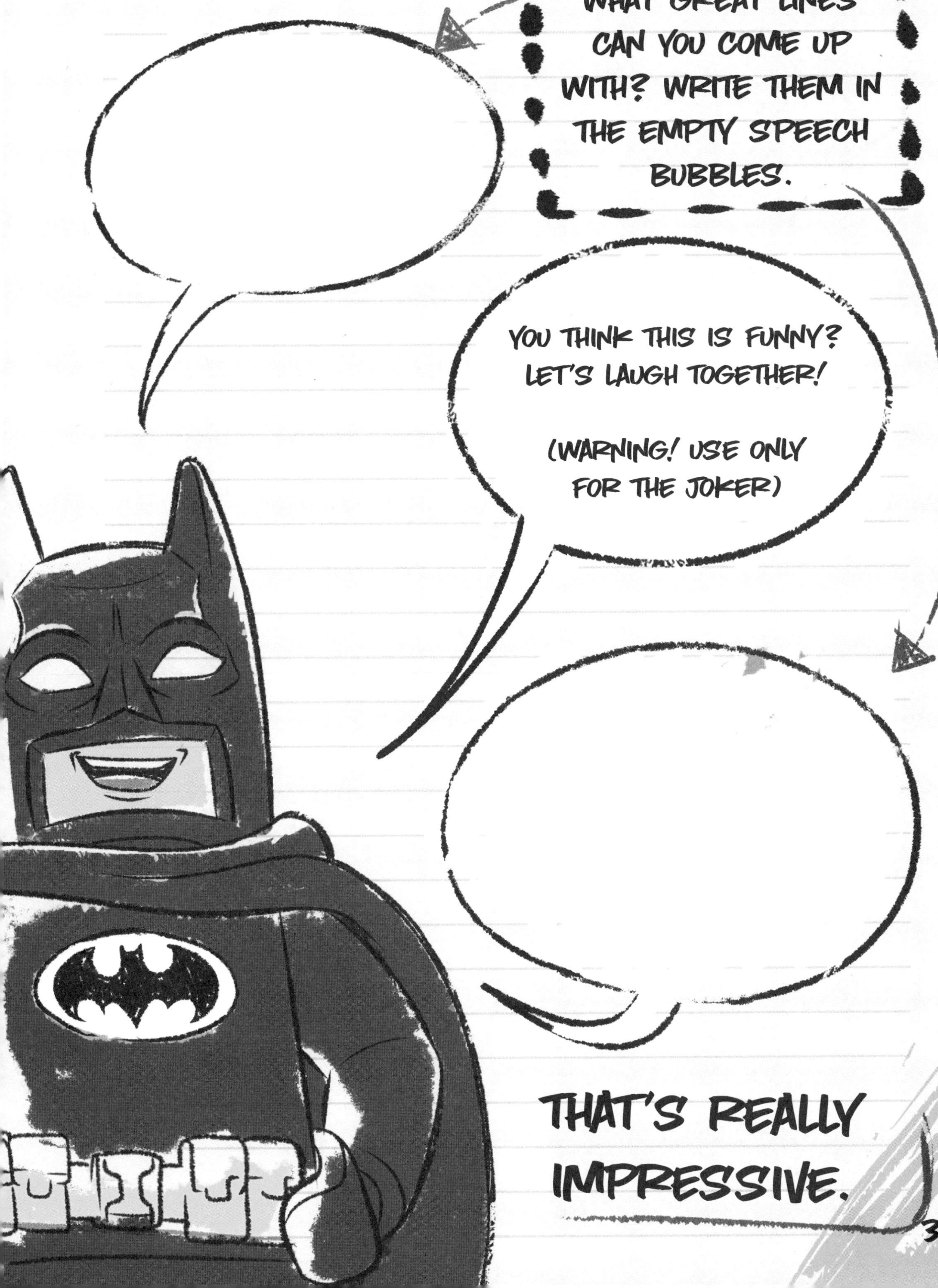
YOU THINK THIS IS FUNNY? LET'S LAUGH TOGETHER!
(WARNING! USE ONLY FOR THE JOKER)

THAT'S REALLY IMPRESSIVE.

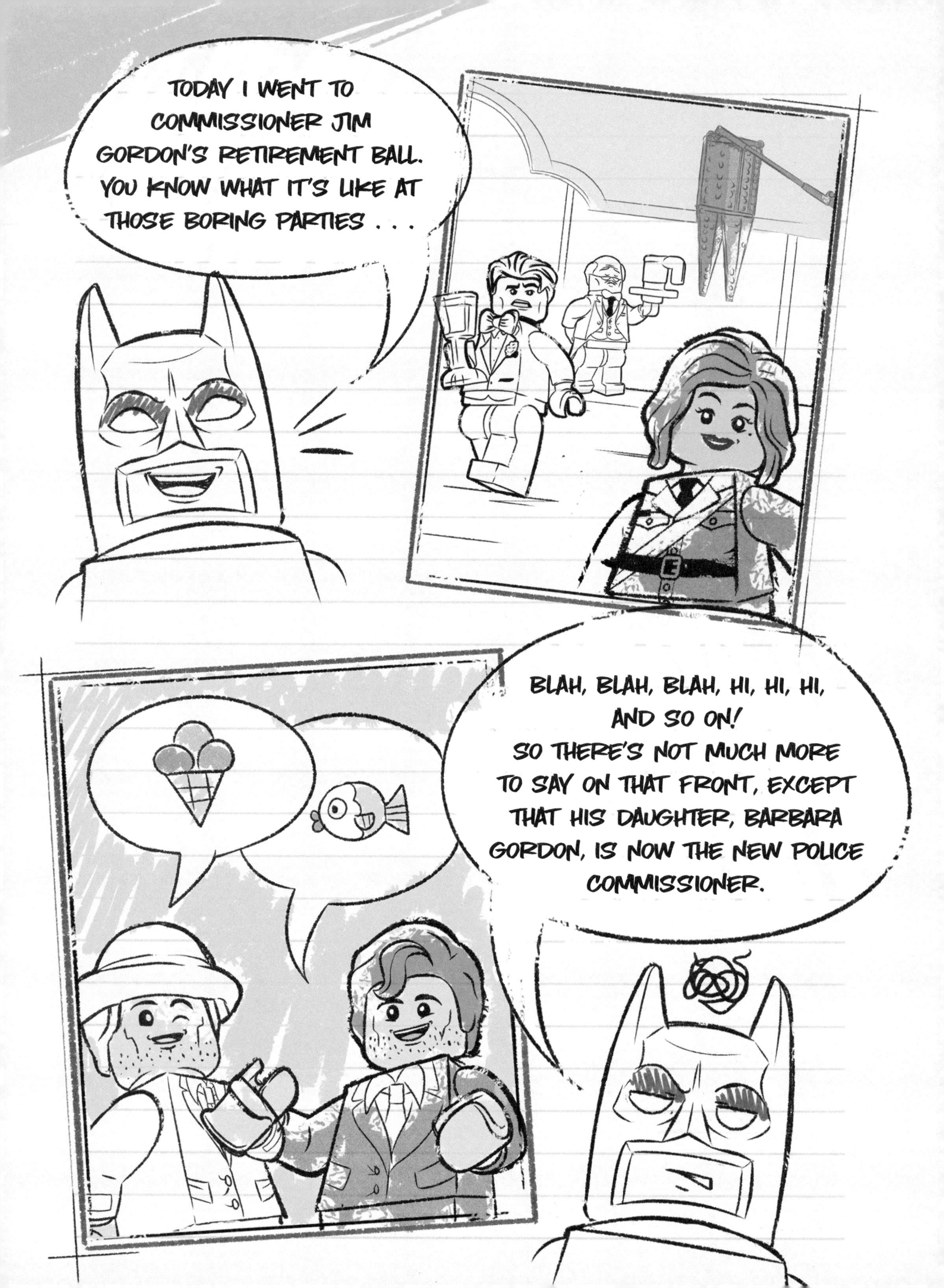
TODAY I WENT TO COMMISSIONER JIM GORDON'S RETIREMENT BALL. YOU KNOW WHAT IT'S LIKE AT THOSE BORING PARTIES . . .
BLAH, BLAH, BLAH, HI, HI, HI, AND SO ON! SO THERE'S NOT MUCH MORE TO SAY ON THAT FRONT, EXCEPT THAT HIS DAUGHTER, BARBARA GORDON, IS NOW THE NEW POLICE COMMISSIONER.

IT'S TIME FOR US TO MAKE THE PARTY A LITTLE MORE EXCITING.

FINISH THE COMIC STRIP, BUT MAKE THE ENDING ON THE NEXT FEW PAGES

REALLY AWESOME!

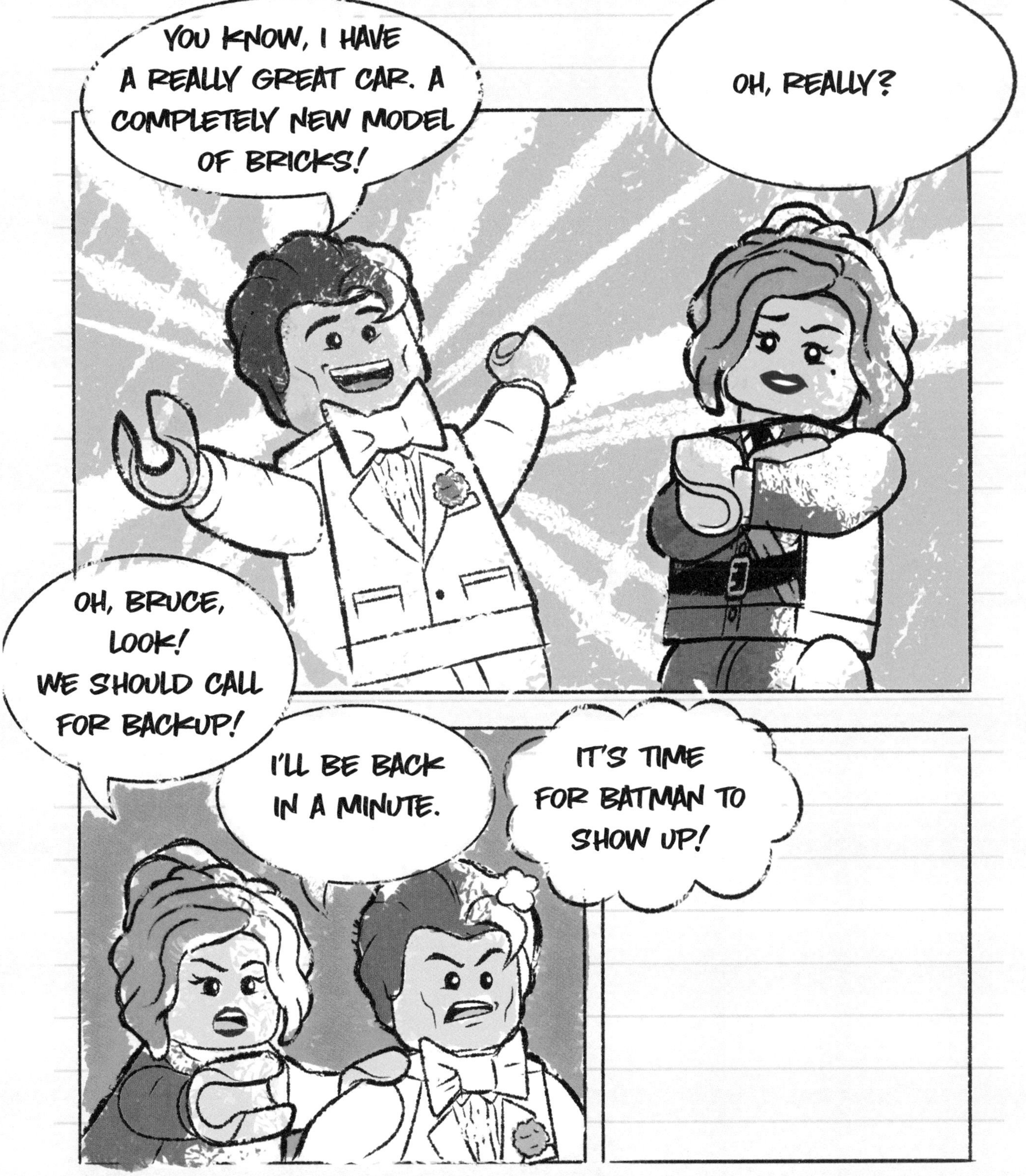
YOU KNOW, I HAVE A REALLY GREAT CAR. A COMPLETELY NEW MODEL OF BRICKS!
OH, REALLY?
OH, BRUCE, LOOK! WE SHOULD CALL FOR BACKUP!
I'LL BE BACK IN A MINUTE.
IT'S TIME FOR BATMAN TO SHOW UP!

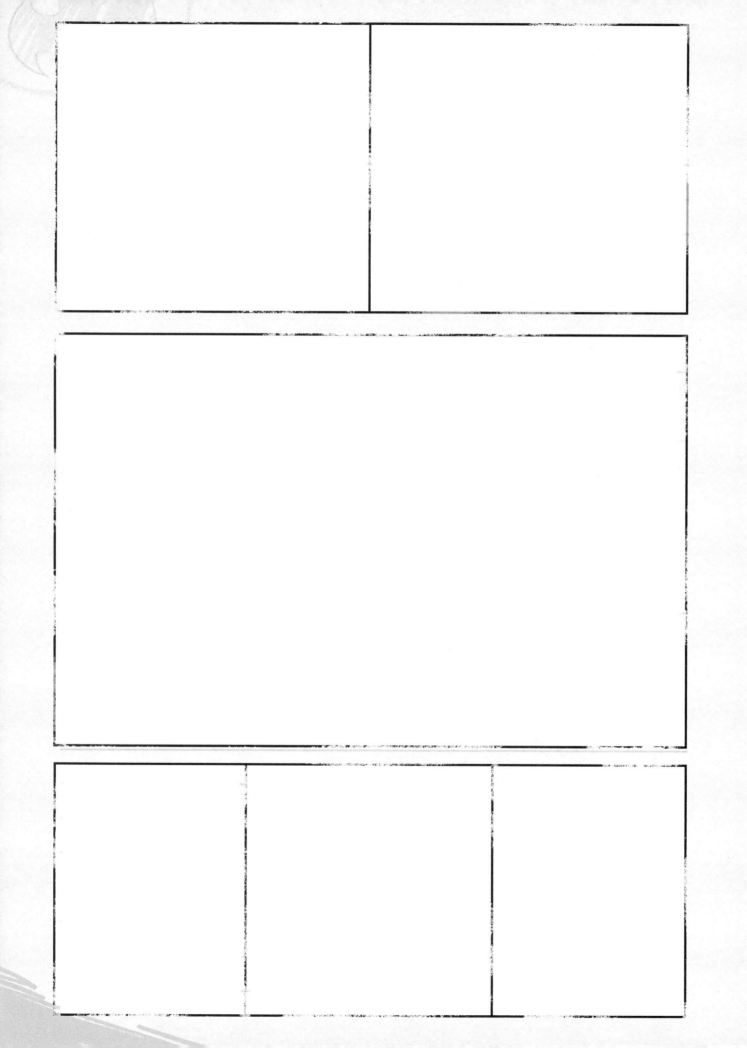

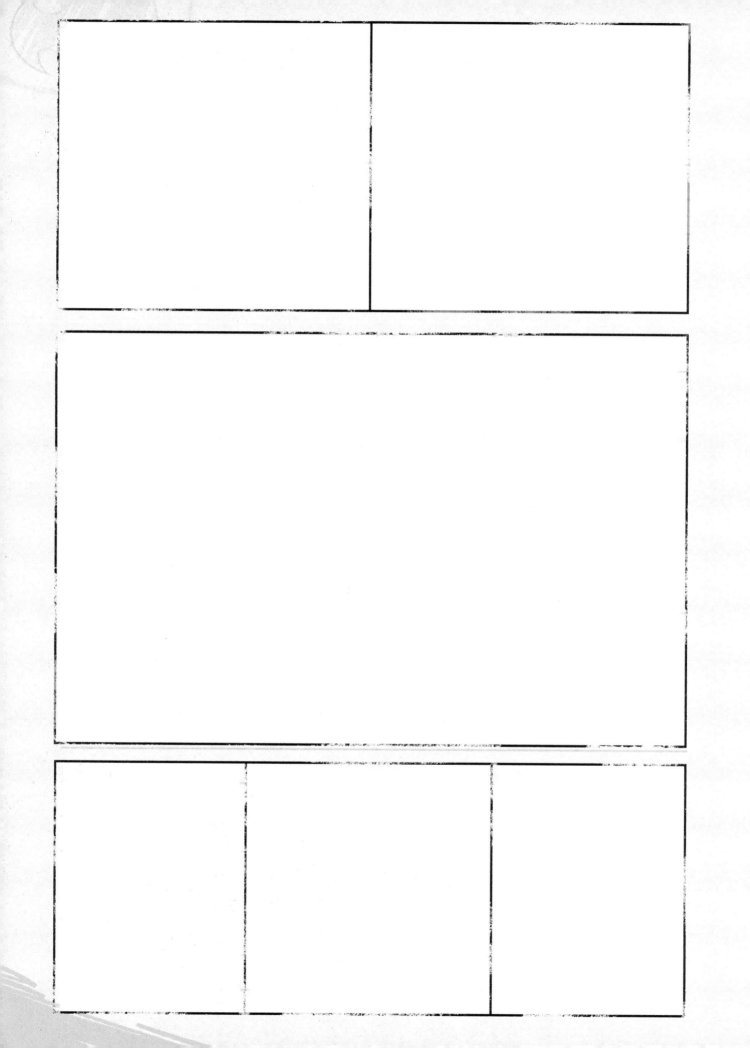

HAS ANYTHING EXCITING HAPPENED TODAY?

WELL, I SAVED THE CITY AGAIN!

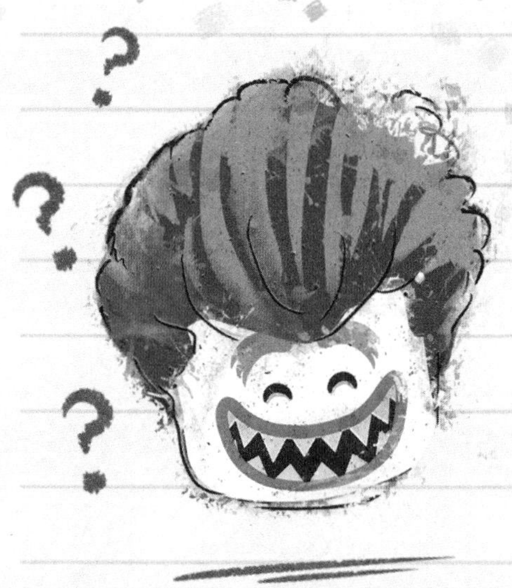

THE JOKER ATTACKED THE CITY. HE BREEZED INTO COMMISSIONER GORDON'S RETIREMENT BALL. HE APPEARED OUT OF THE BLUE.

AND, AS USUAL, HE PUT ON AN ACT!

BRUCE WAYNE NEEDED TO BECOME BATMAN!

AND JUST WHEN I WAS ABOUT TO TRY MY NEW . . .

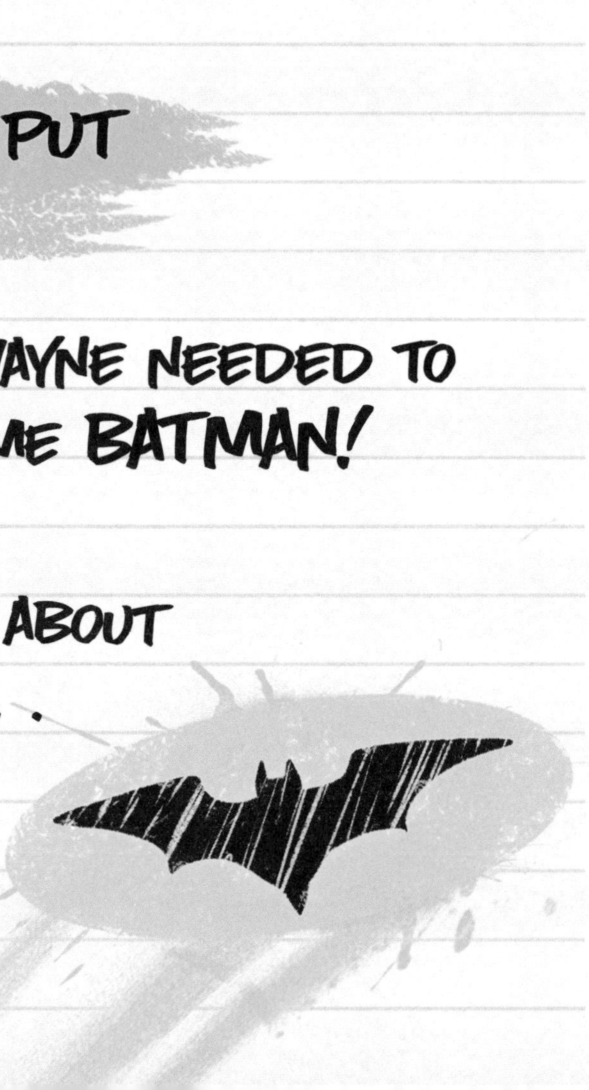

BAM,

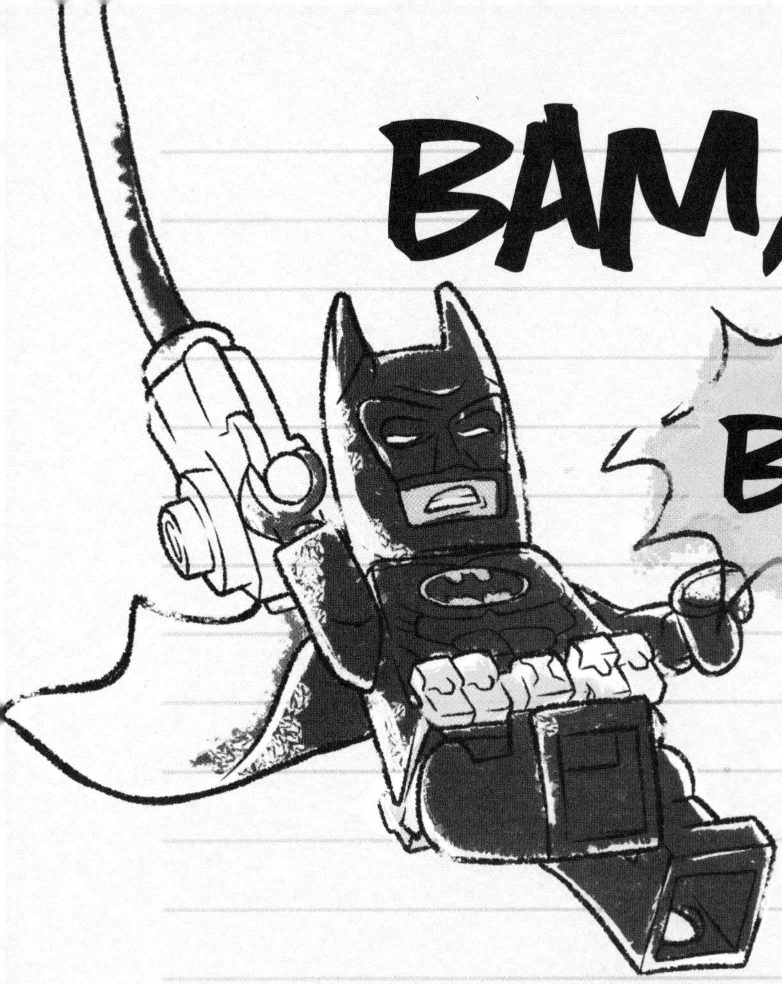

BOOM,

!!!

KICK

AND WHAM ON HIM . . .

HE SUDDENLY SURRENDERED!

? ?

HOLD ON, SOMETHING'S NOT RIGHT HERE . . . THE JOKER WOULDN'T NORMALLY SURRENDER WITHOUT A FIGHT. WHAT'S GOING ON?

THE JOKER HAS CROSSED PATHS WITH ME TOO MANY TIMES . . .

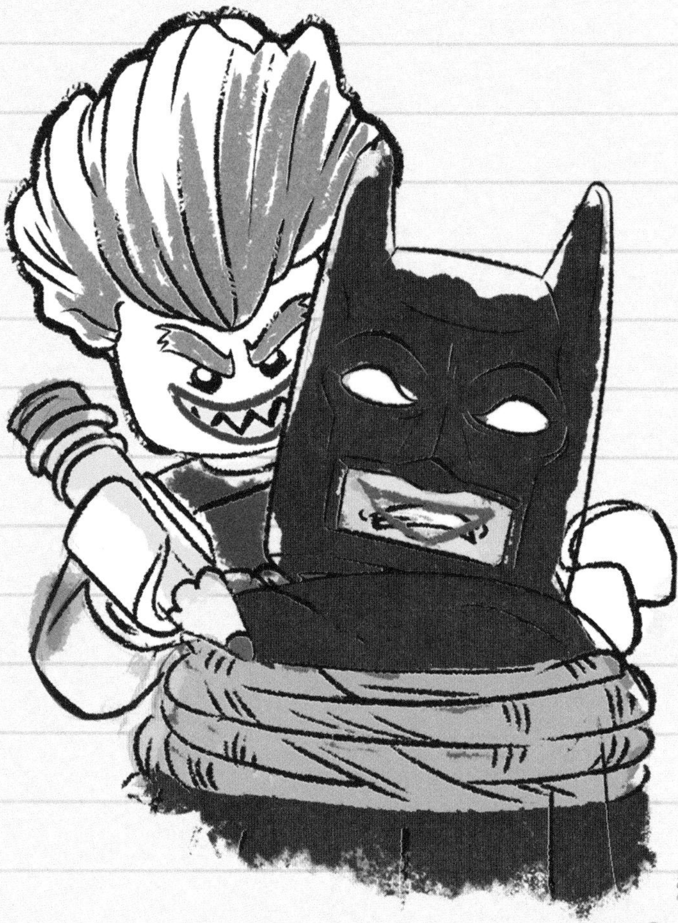

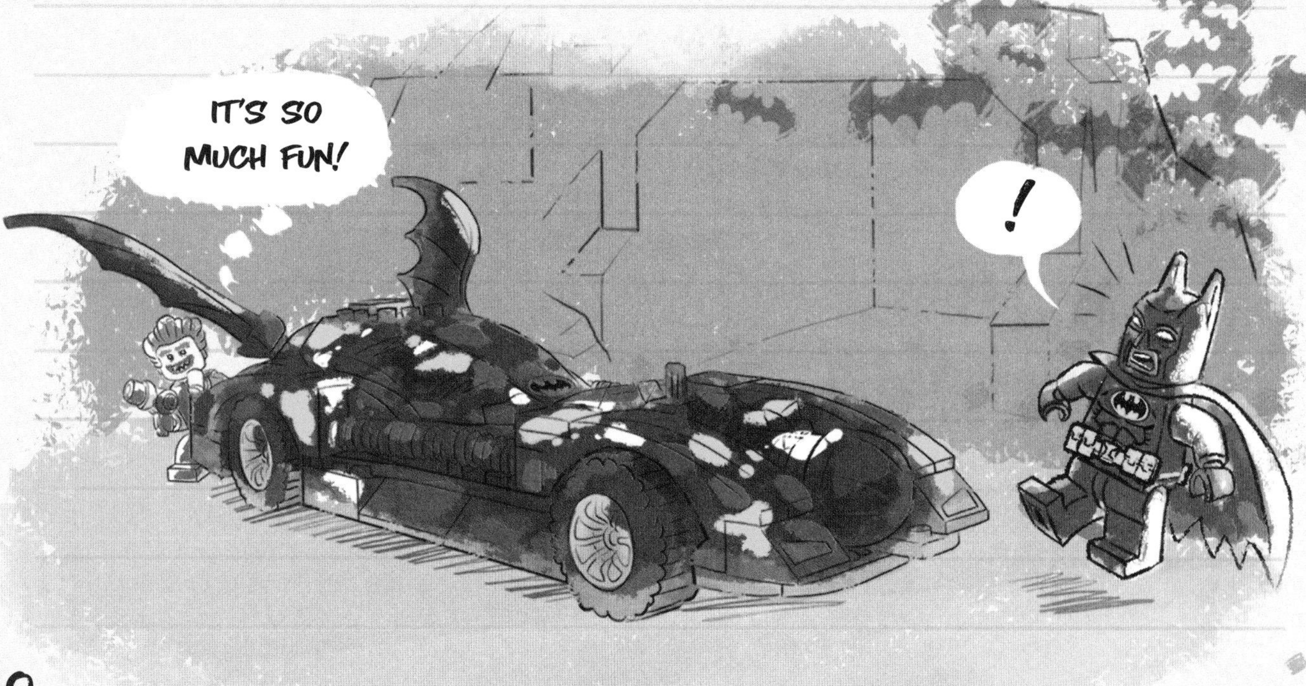
IT'S SO MUCH FUN!
!

DRAW THE JOKER GETTING ON MY NERVES **HERE!**

BUT IT'S ALWAYS **FUN** IN THE END!

!!!

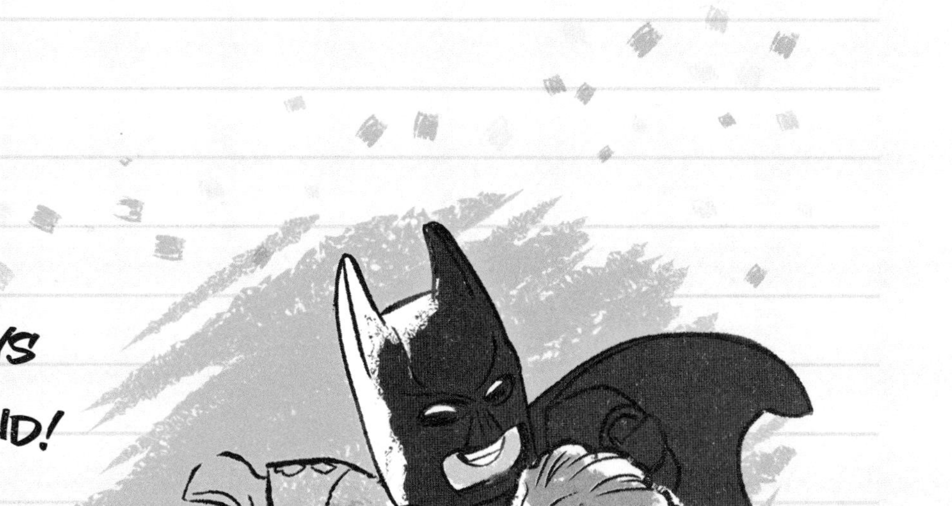

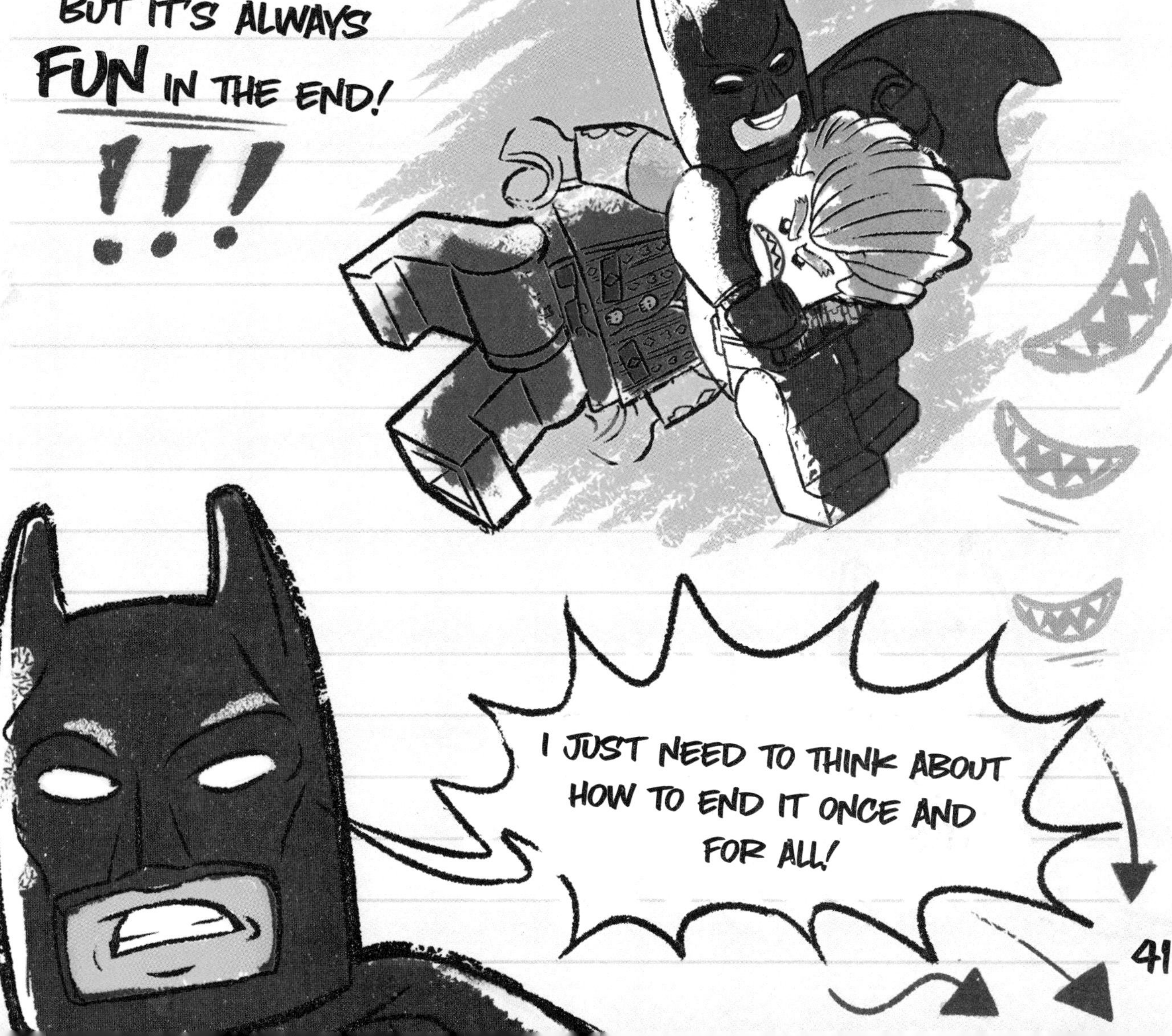
I JUST NEED TO THINK ABOUT HOW TO END IT ONCE AND FOR ALL!

I'M A TALENTED ARTIST!

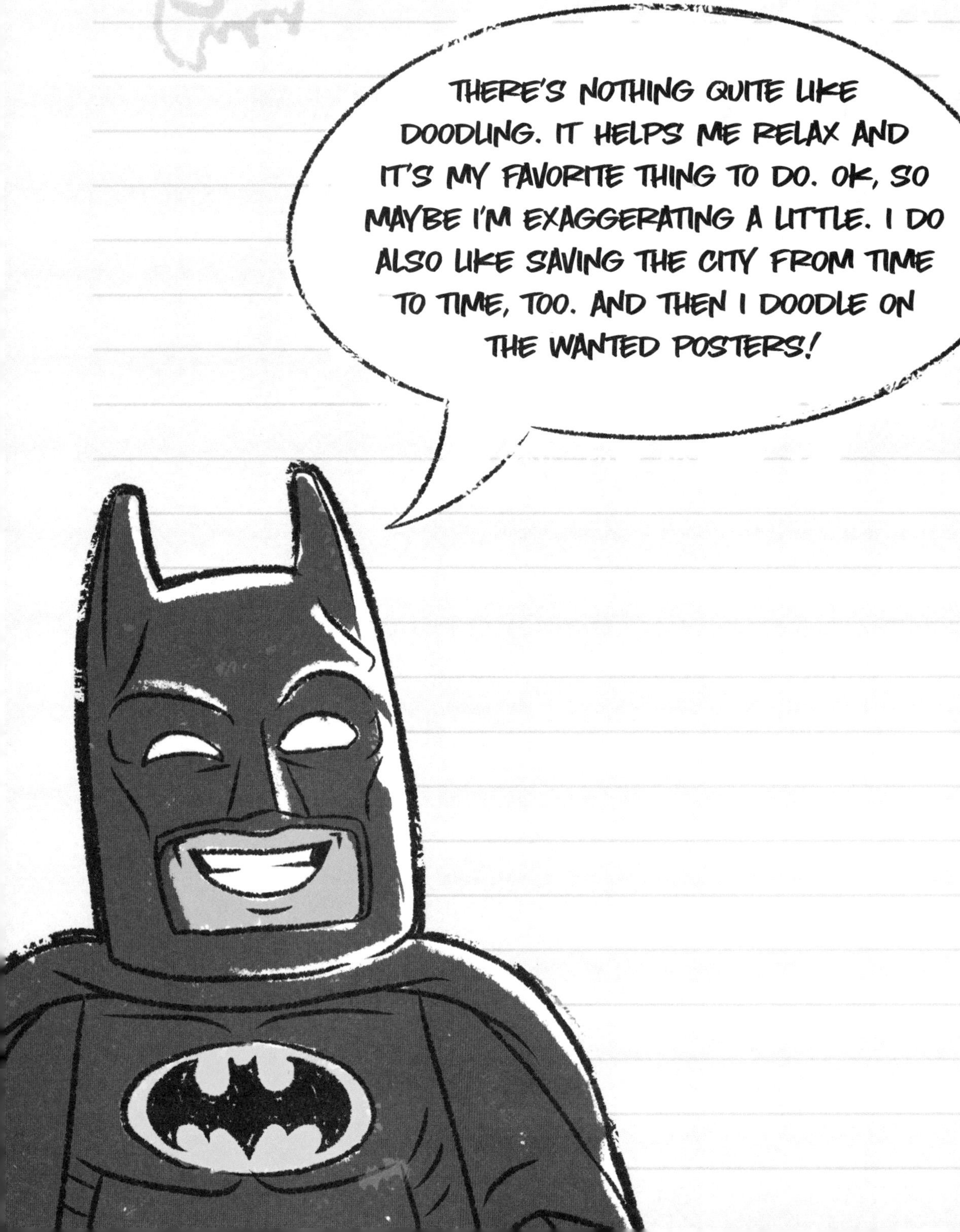
THERE'S NOTHING QUITE LIKE DOODLING. IT HELPS ME RELAX AND IT'S MY FAVORITE THING TO DO. OK, SO MAYBE I'M EXAGGERATING A LITTLE. I DO ALSO LIKE SAVING THE CITY FROM TIME TO TIME, TOO. AND THEN I DOODLE ON THE WANTED POSTERS!

WANTED

NOW IT'S YOUR TURN TO DOODLE ON THE POSTERS OF THE UNLUCKY ONES WHO DARED TO CROSS PATHS WITH ME!

WANTED

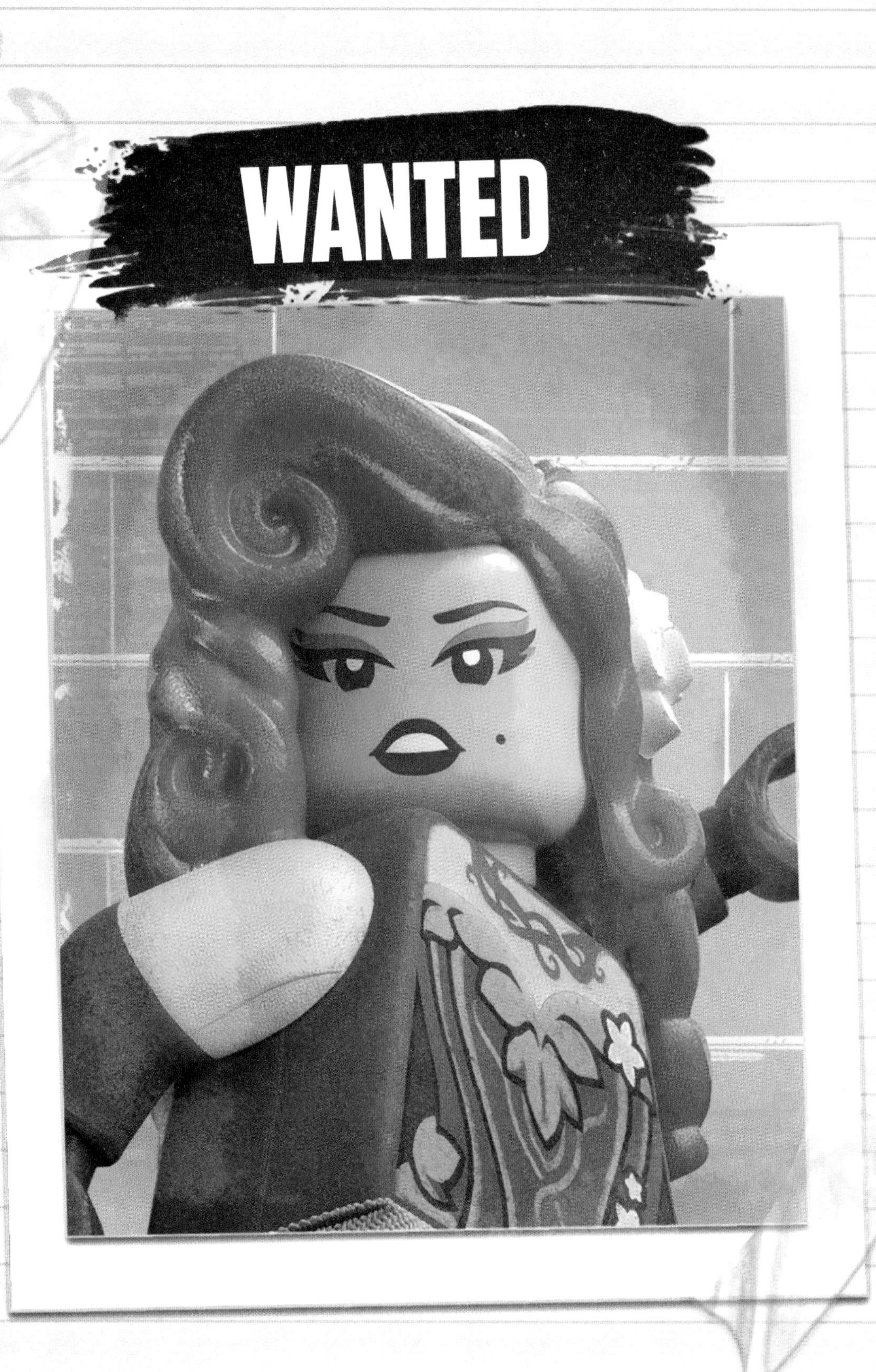

WANTED

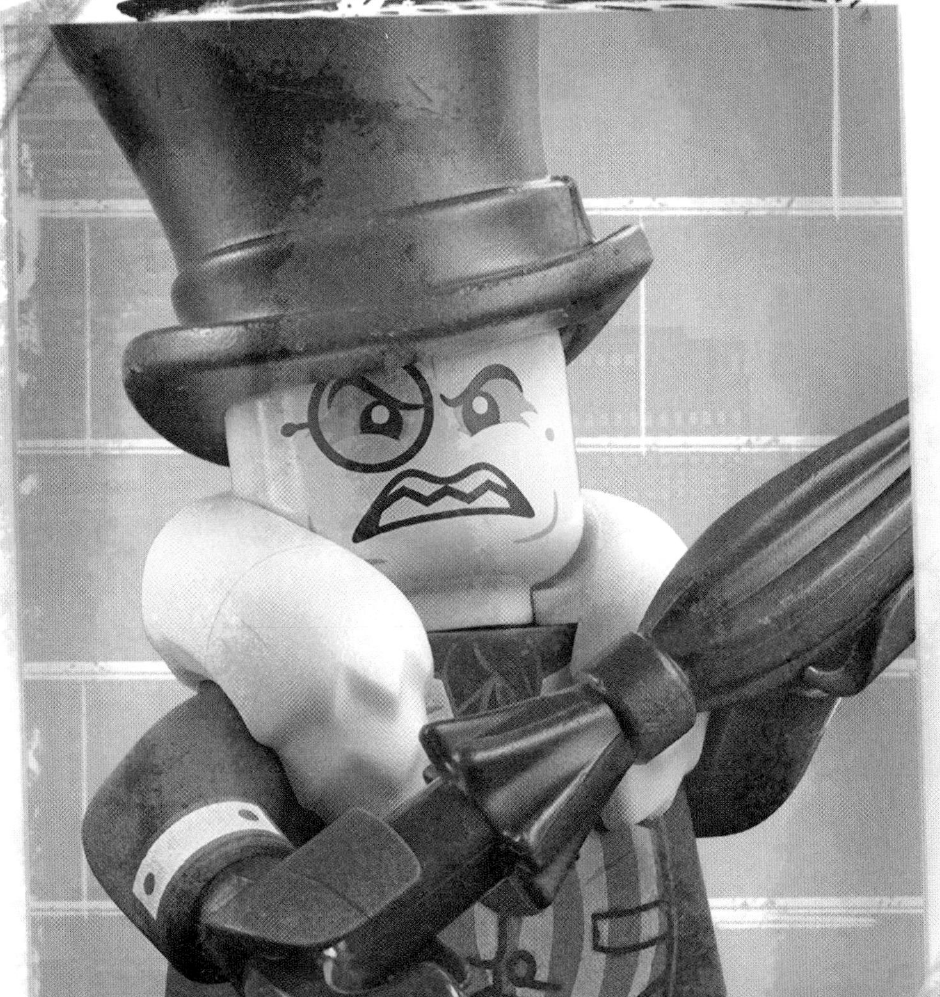

WANTED

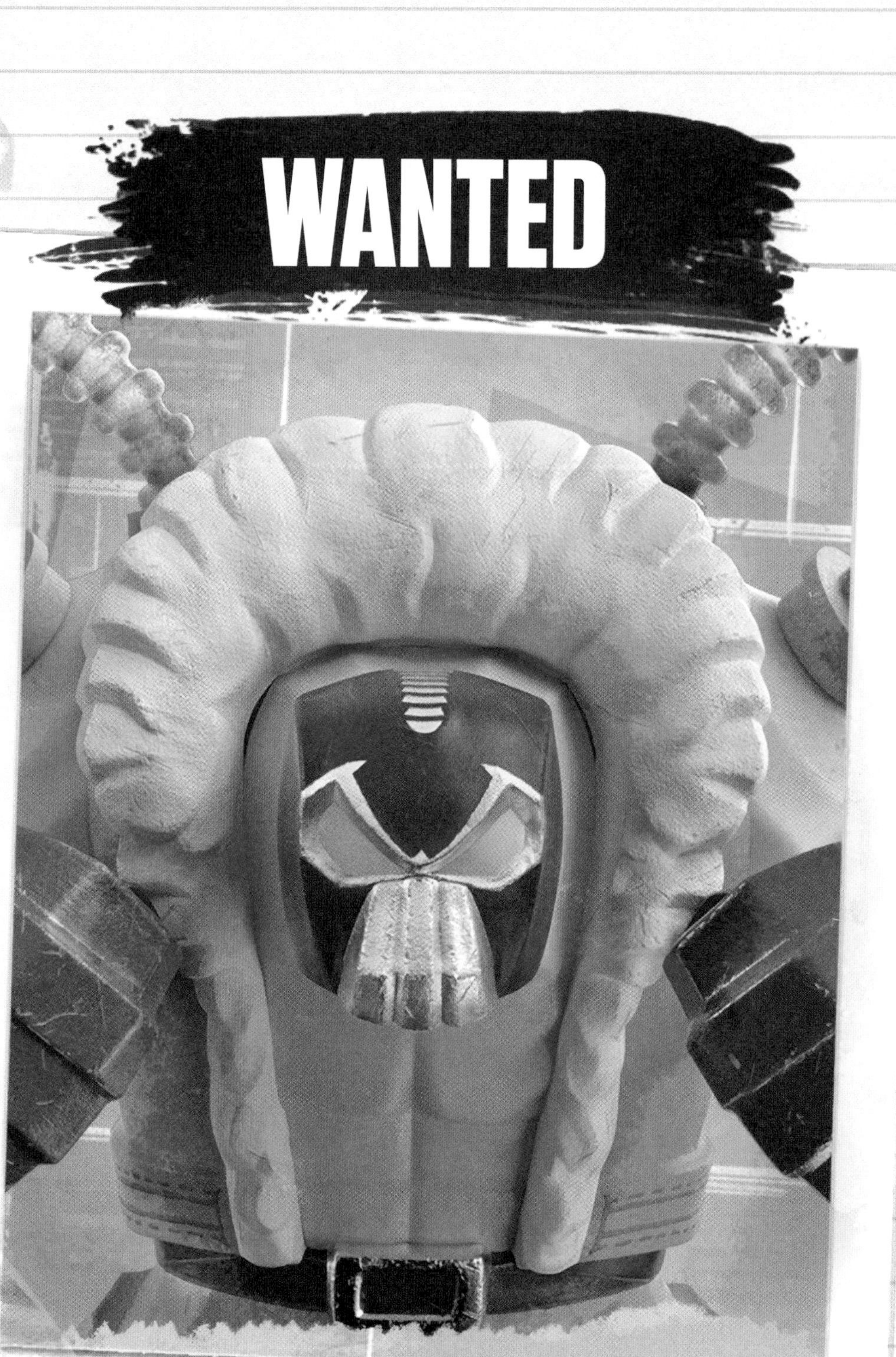

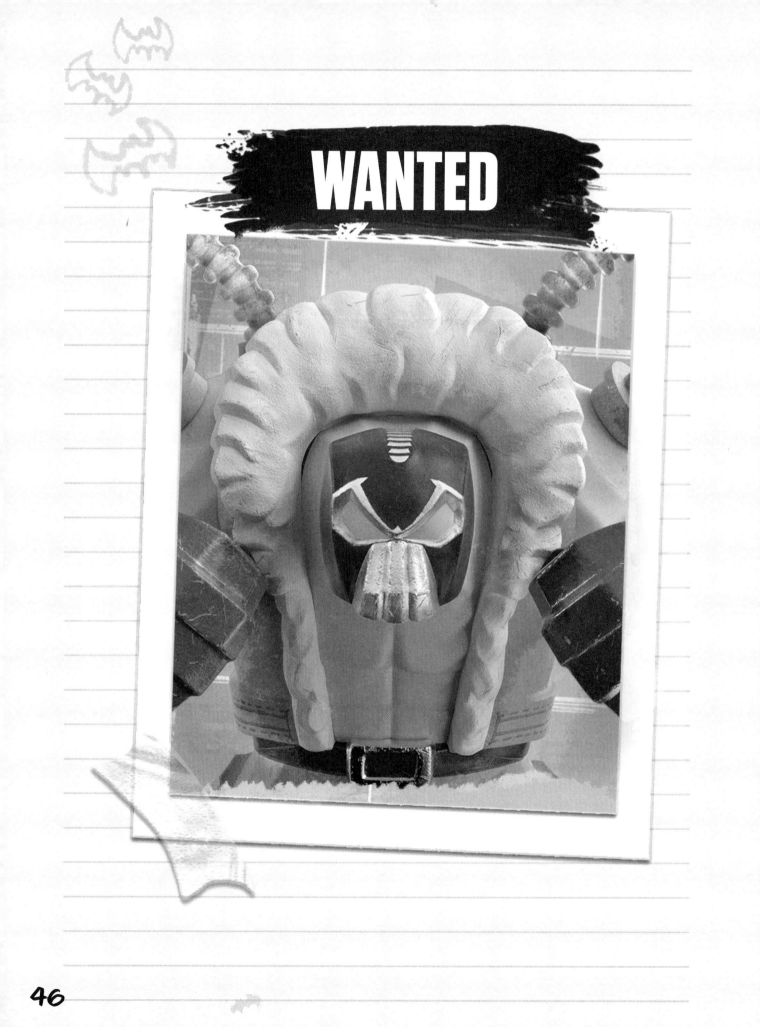

WANTED

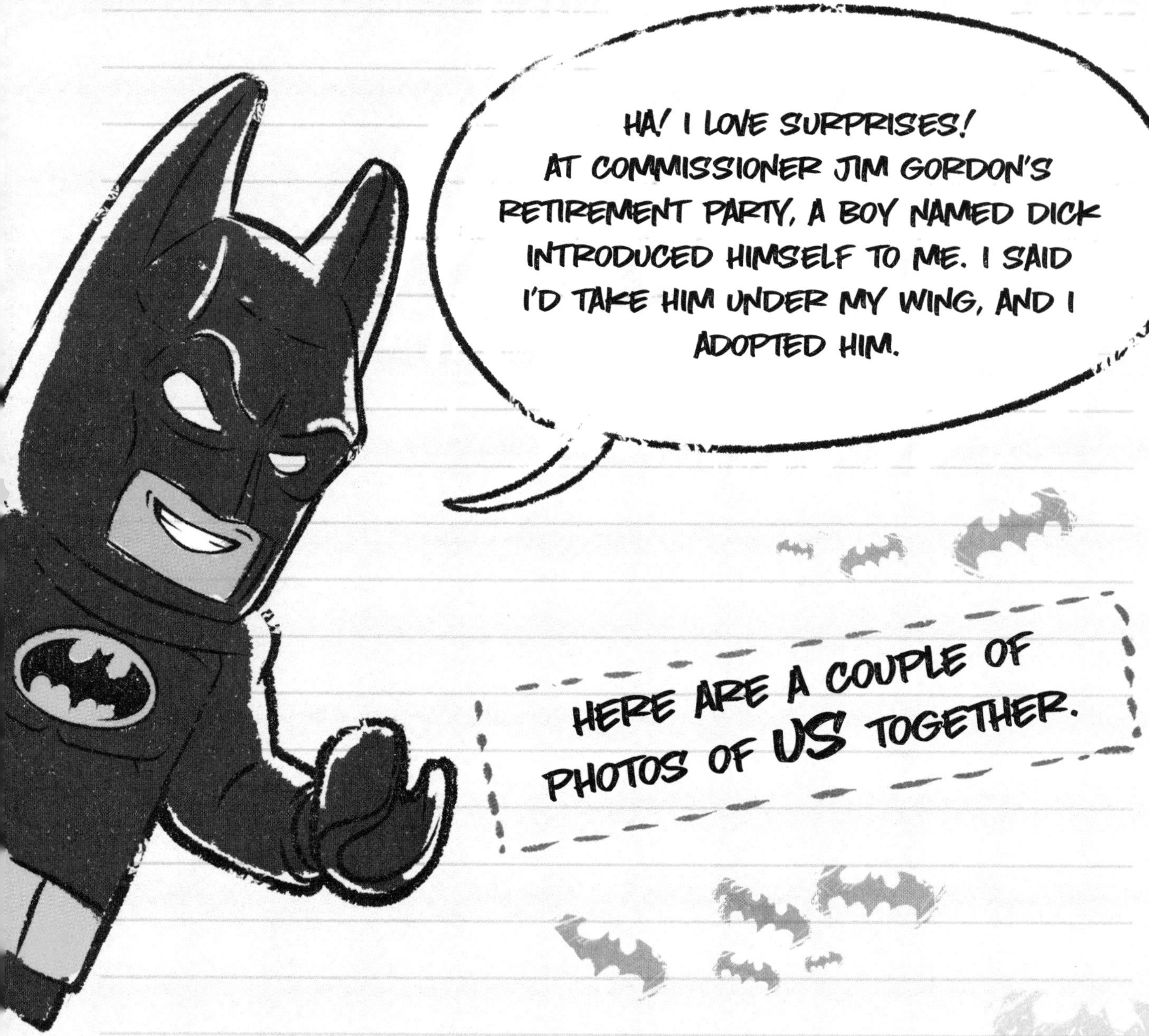
HA! I LOVE SURPRISES! AT COMMISSIONER JIM GORDON'S RETIREMENT PARTY, A BOY NAMED DICK INTRODUCED HIMSELF TO ME. I SAID I'D TAKE HIM UNDER MY WING, AND I ADOPTED HIM.
HERE ARE A COUPLE OF PHOTOS OF US! TOGETHER.

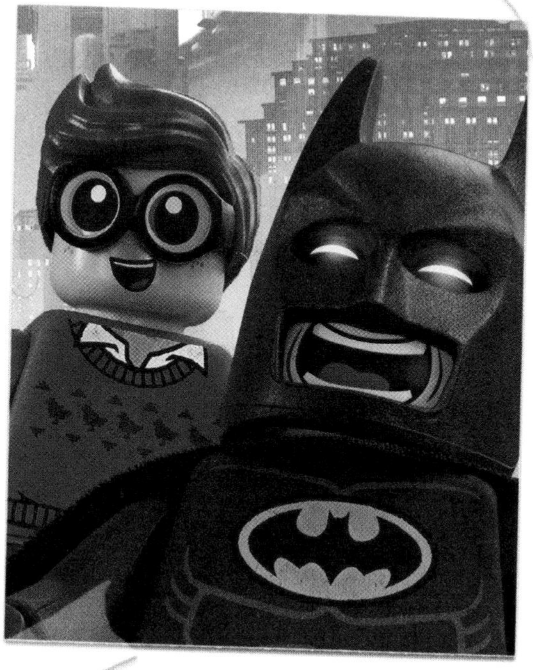

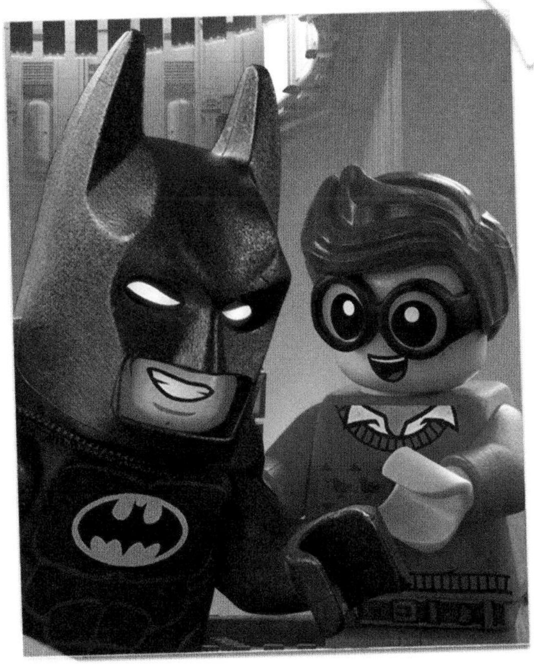

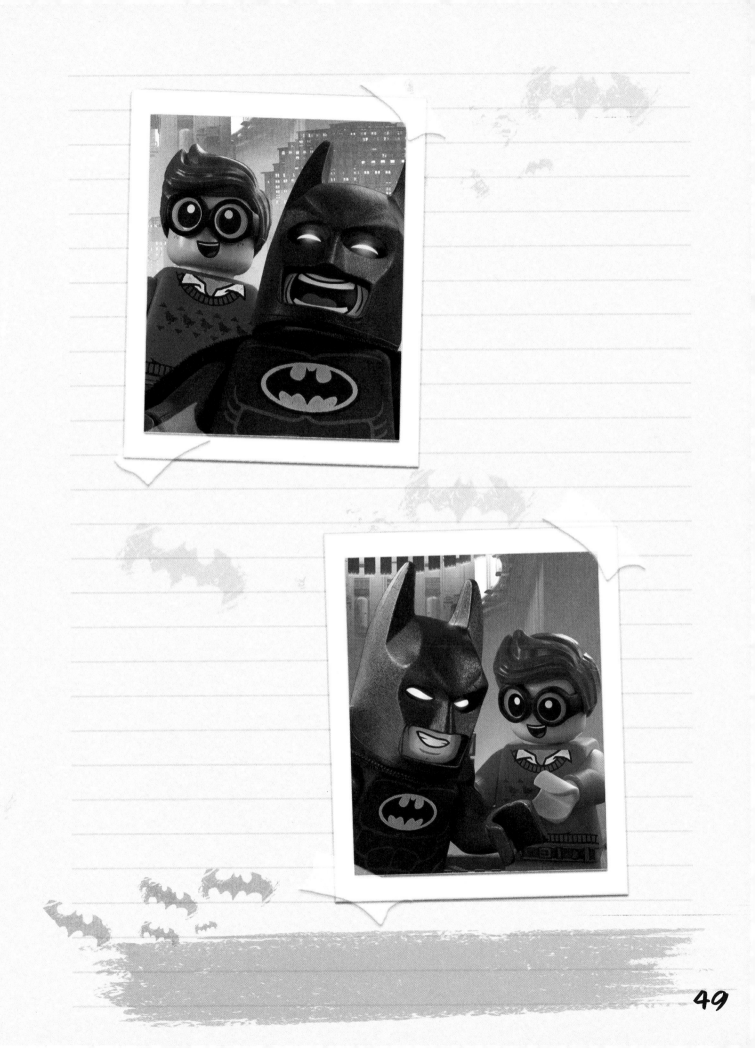

Can you draw us posing in some more pics?

I DO **LOVE** A SELFIE OR TWO, OR THREE OR MORE!

DICK STILL THINKS THAT BATMAN AND BRUCE WAYNE ARE TWO DIFFERENT PEOPLE! OH WELL!

HOW TO BE A SUPER HERO

PART 1 (THEORY)

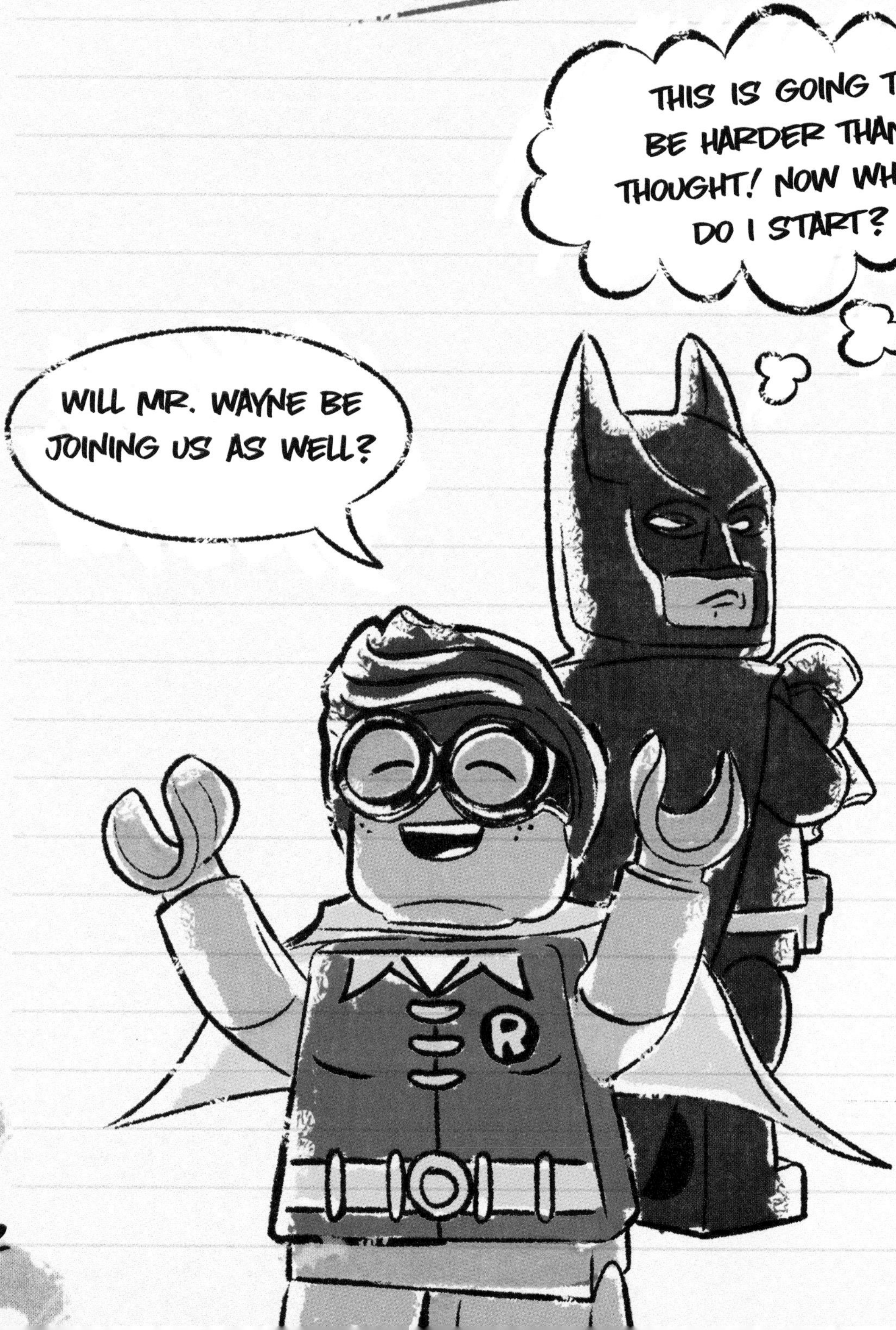
THIS IS GOING TO BE HARDER THAN I THOUGHT! NOW WHERE DO I START?
WILL MR. WAYNE BE JOINING US AS WELL?

WHAT ARE THE FIRST THINGS YOU NEED TO DO AS A YOUNG SUPER HERO?

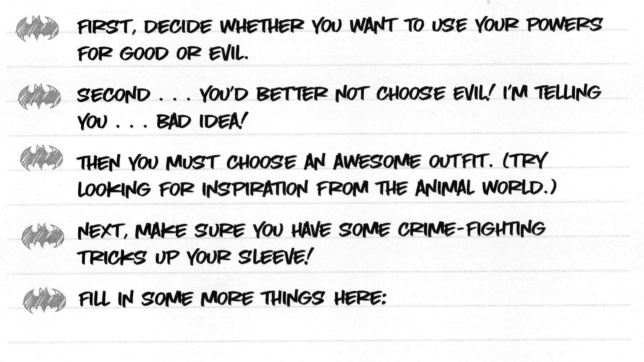

- FIRST, DECIDE WHETHER YOU WANT TO USE YOUR POWERS FOR GOOD OR EVIL.

- SECOND . . . YOU'D BETTER NOT CHOOSE EVIL! I'M TELLING YOU . . . BAD IDEA!

- THEN YOU MUST CHOOSE AN AWESOME OUTFIT. (TRY LOOKING FOR INSPIRATION FROM THE ANIMAL WORLD.)

- NEXT, MAKE SURE YOU HAVE SOME CRIME-FIGHTING TRICKS UP YOUR SLEEVE!

- FILL IN SOME MORE THINGS HERE:

SOMETIMES I THINK ABOUT HOW **MYSTERIOUS** I AM.

I'M BATMAN, A SUPER HERO WITH A HEART FULL OF SECRETS AND **DARKNESS**.

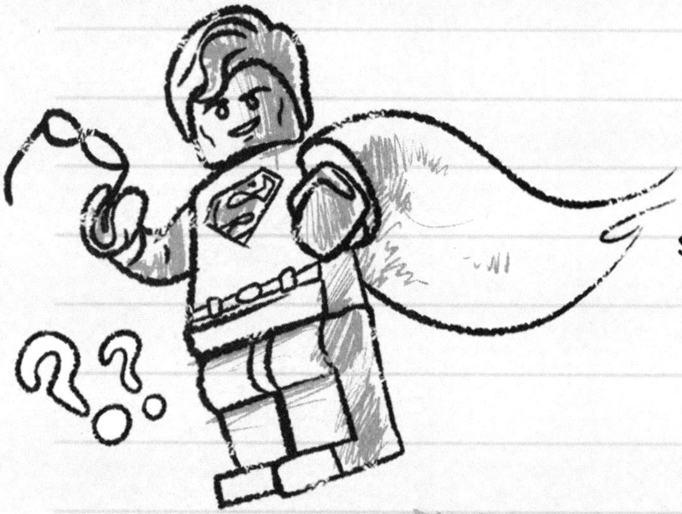

SURELY THERE COULDN'T BE **ANYTHING** MORE MYSTERIOUS OUT THERE . . .

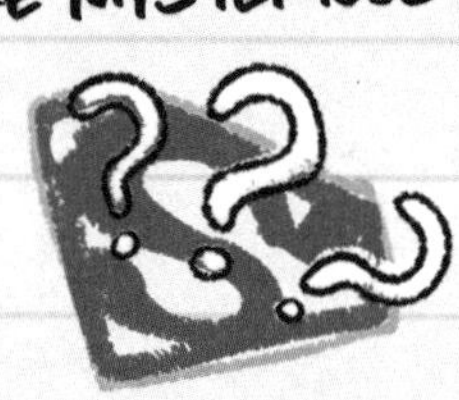

EXCEPT FOR THE **MYSTERY** OF WHY NOBODY RECOGNIZES THAT **CLARK KENT** IS **SUPERMAN!**

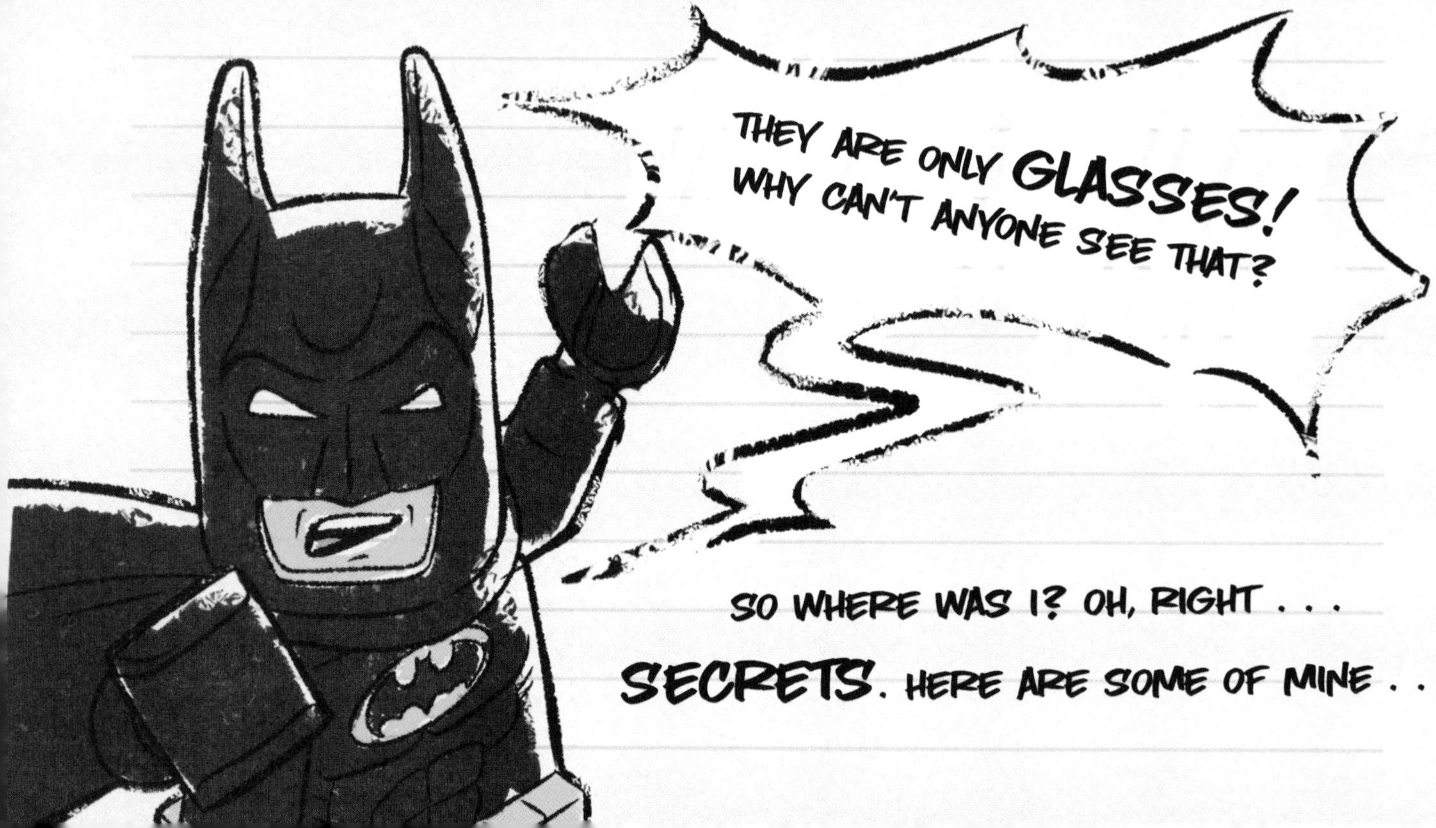
THEY ARE ONLY GLASSES! WHY CAN'T ANYONE SEE THAT?

SO WHERE WAS I? OH, RIGHT . . .

SECRETS. HERE ARE SOME OF MINE . . .

SECRET 1
(A SMALL ONE)

ONE POCKET IN MY UTILITY BELT IS FOR SPARE SOCKS!

SECRET 2

I'D LIKE TO CARVE THE BATMAN SYMBOL ON TO THE SIDE OF THE MOON AND THEN SEE THE LOOK ON THE JOKER'S FACE!

SECRET 3
(THE BIGGEST ONE)

WHEN I STAY IN THE BATCAVE TOO LONG, I LOSE TRACK OF WHETHER IT'S DAY OR NIGHT, AND I START FEELING A BIT LONELY . . .

BUT DON'T WORRY, I GET OVER IT BY HANGING WITH MY BAT FRIENDS!

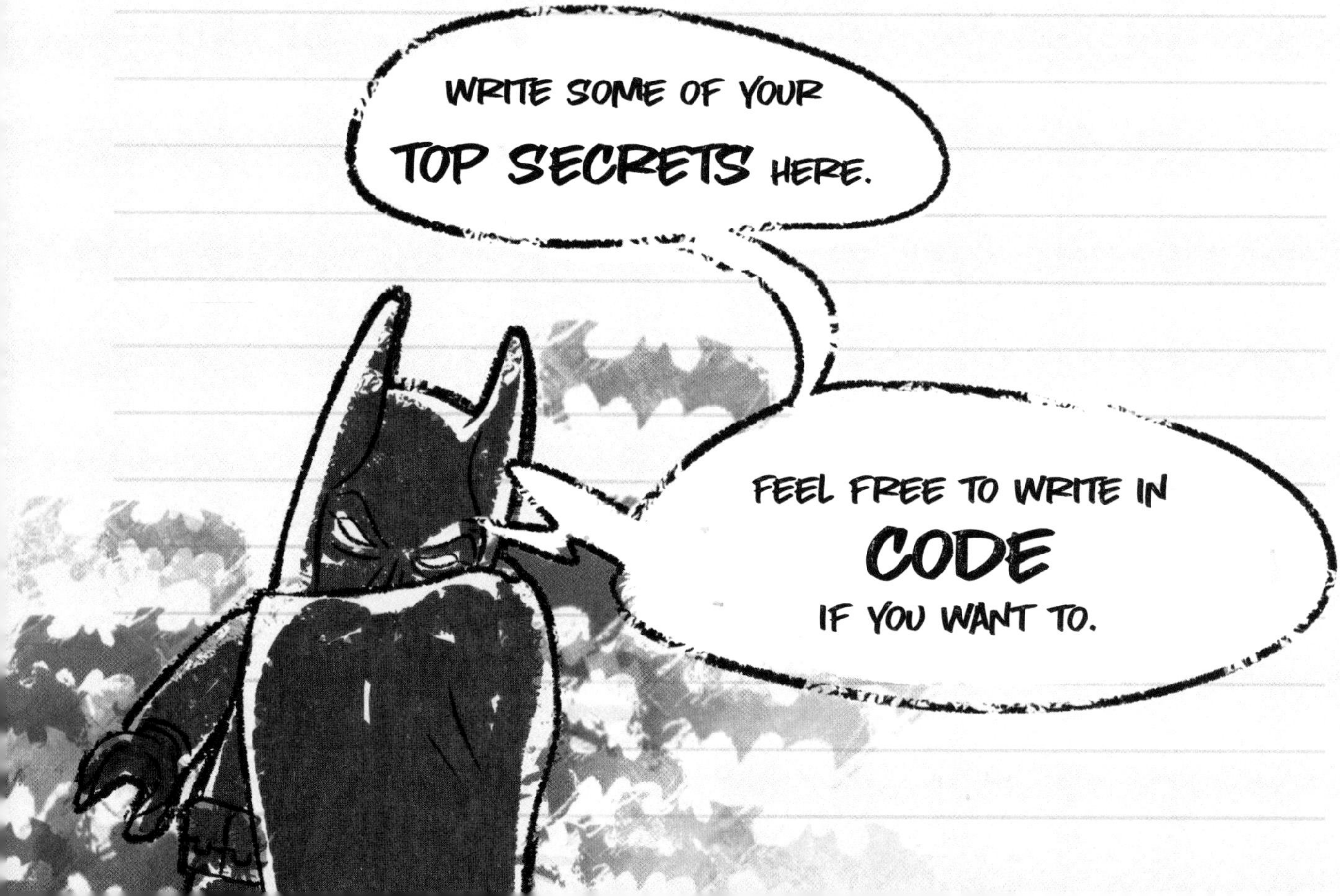
WRITE SOME OF YOUR TOP SECRETS HERE.
FEEL FREE TO WRITE IN CODE IF YOU WANT TO.

I HAVE JUST REALIZED THAT

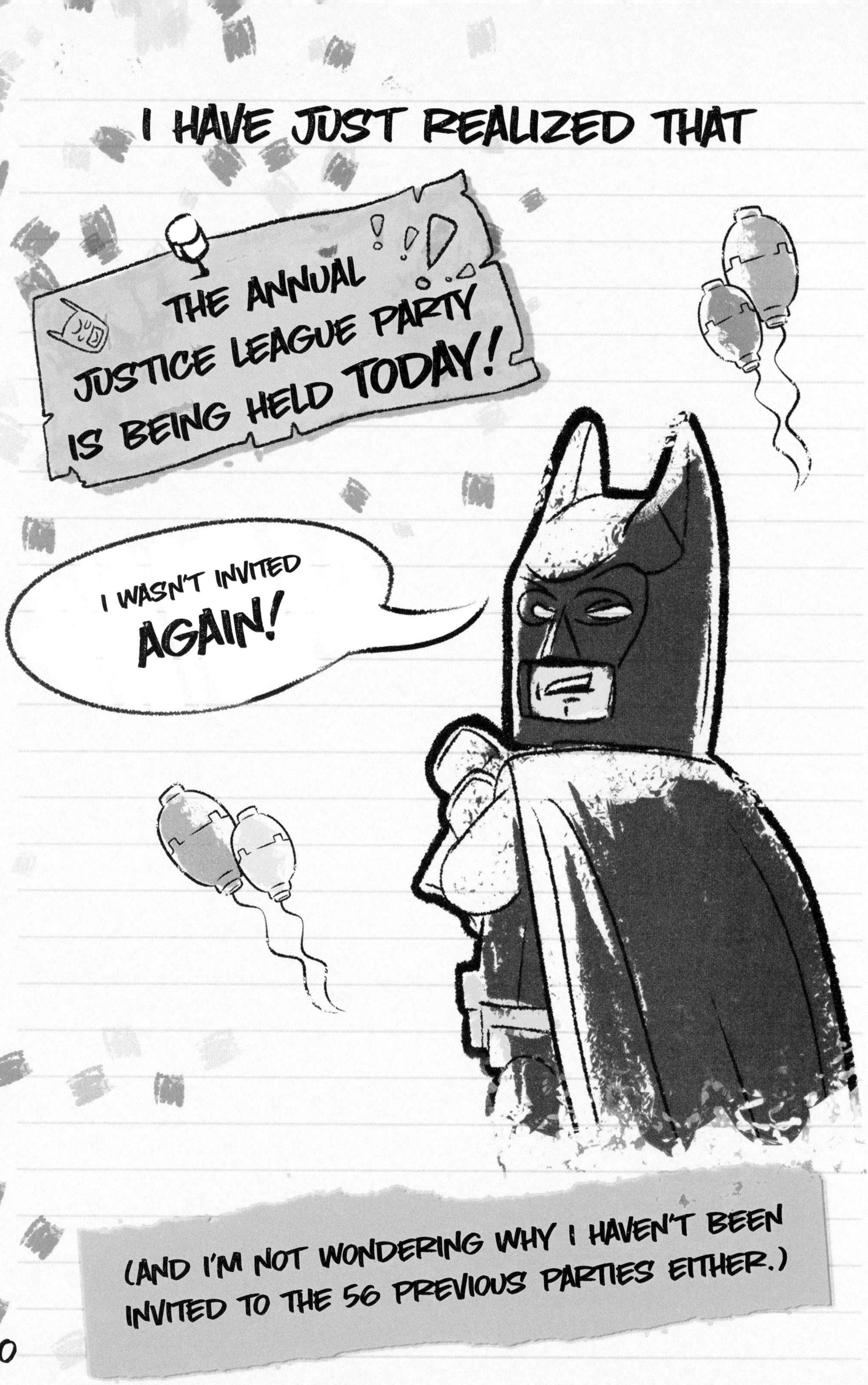
THE ANNUAL JUSTICE LEAGUE PARTY IS BEING HELD TODAY!
I WASN'T INVITED AGAIN!

(AND I'M NOT WONDERING WHY I HAVEN'T BEEN INVITED TO THE 56 PREVIOUS PARTIES EITHER.)

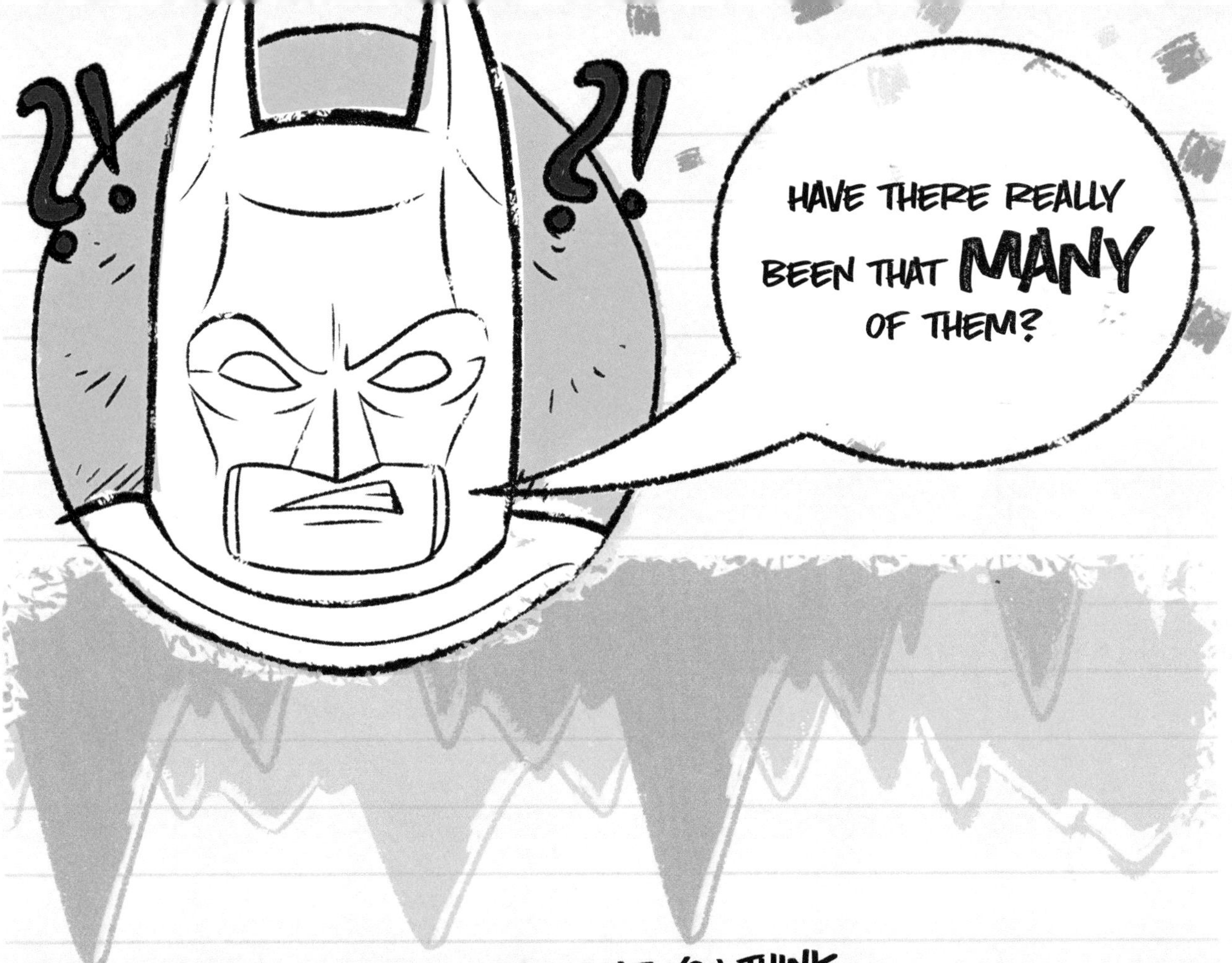
?!
?!
HAVE THERE REALLY BEEN THAT MANY OF THEM?

WRITE IN THE SPACE BELOW WHAT YOU THINK **SUPERMAN** AND THE **FLASH** WOULD SAY ABOUT BATMAN NOT BEING INVITED.

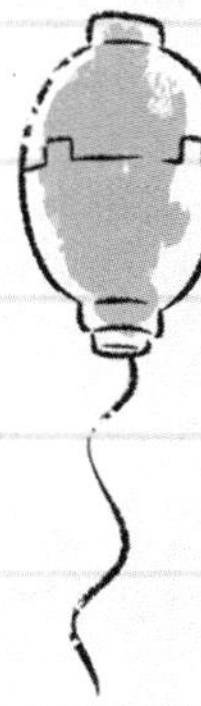

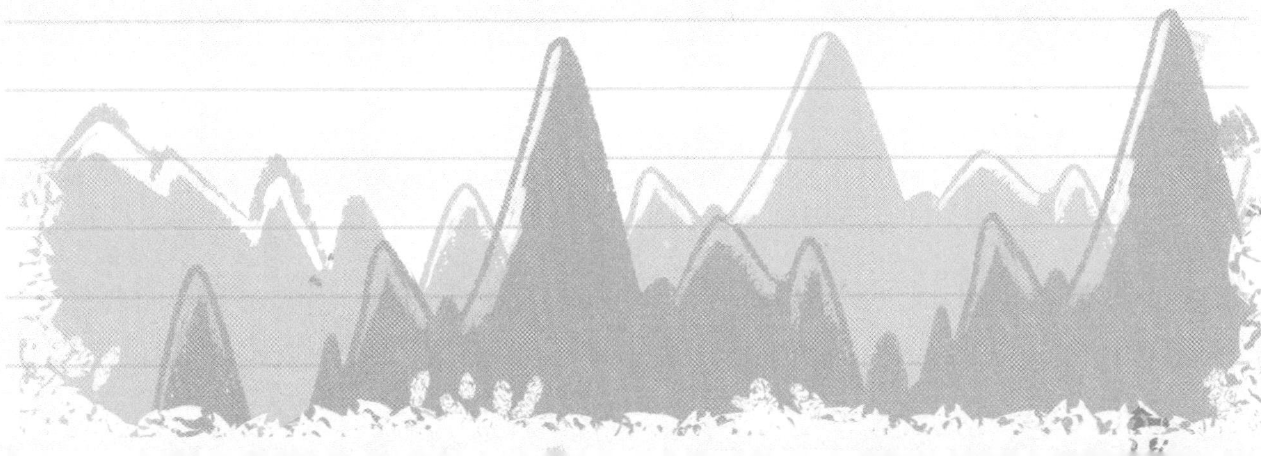

Use all your skills to prepare a cool **JUSTICE LEAGUE** party invitation just for me!

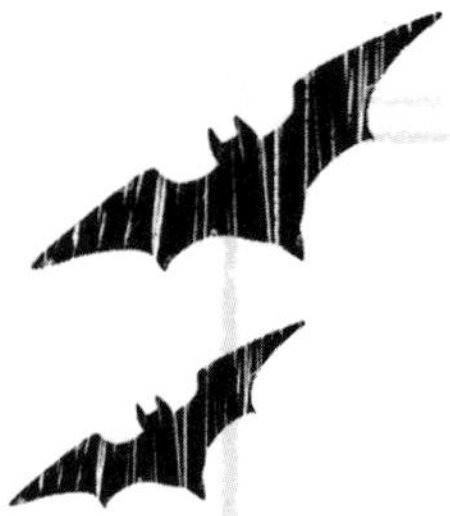

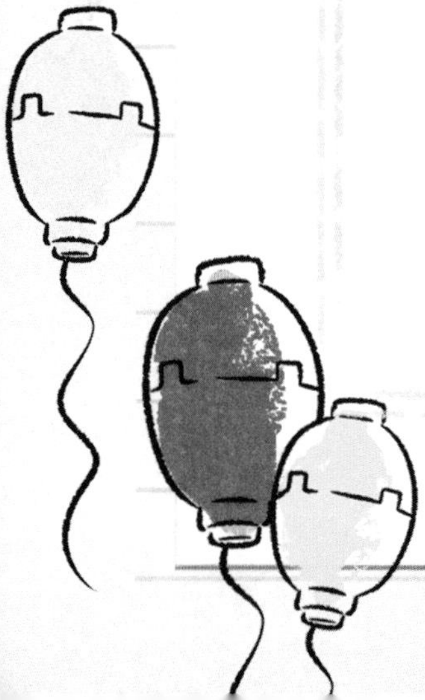

I PREDICT THAT **BARBARA GORDON**,
GOTHAM'S NEW POLICE COMMISSIONER,

IS GOING TO BE **BATGIRL**

AND MY INTUITION IS NEVER WRONG.

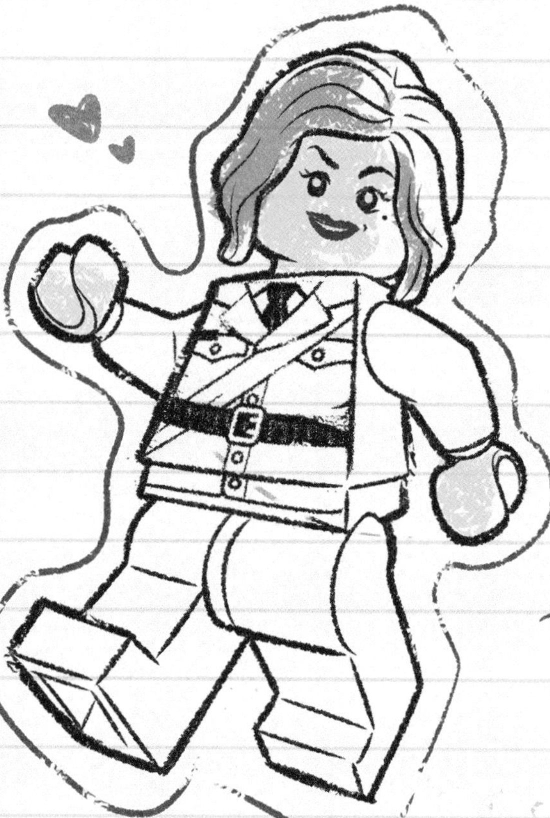

BARBARA WILL
TRANSFORM INTO . . .
BATGIRL!

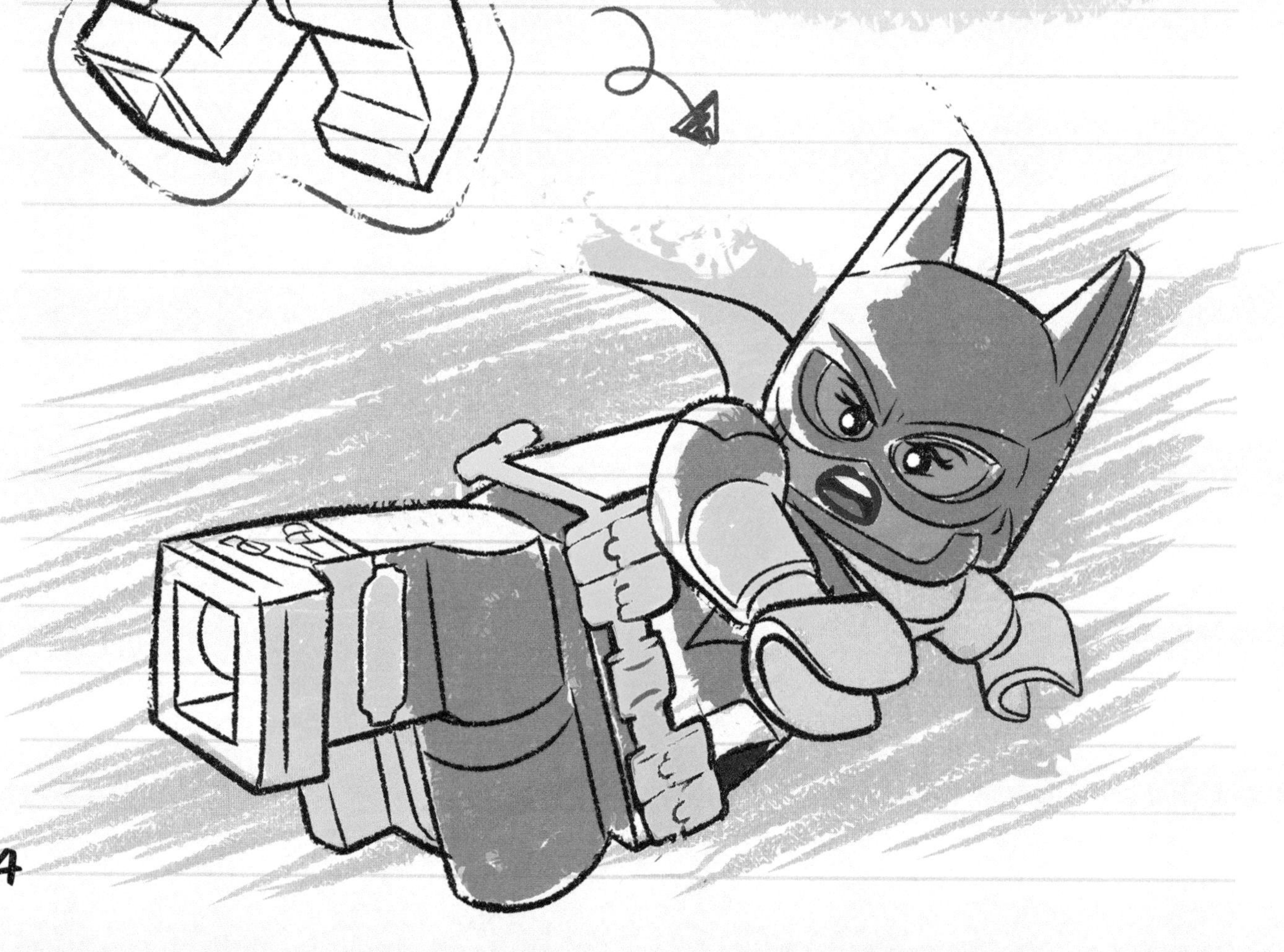

LOOK AT BARBARA'S OUTFITS.
CAN YOU DESIGN ANOTHER ONE FOR HER?

HOW TO BE A SUPER HERO

PART 2 (PRACTICE)

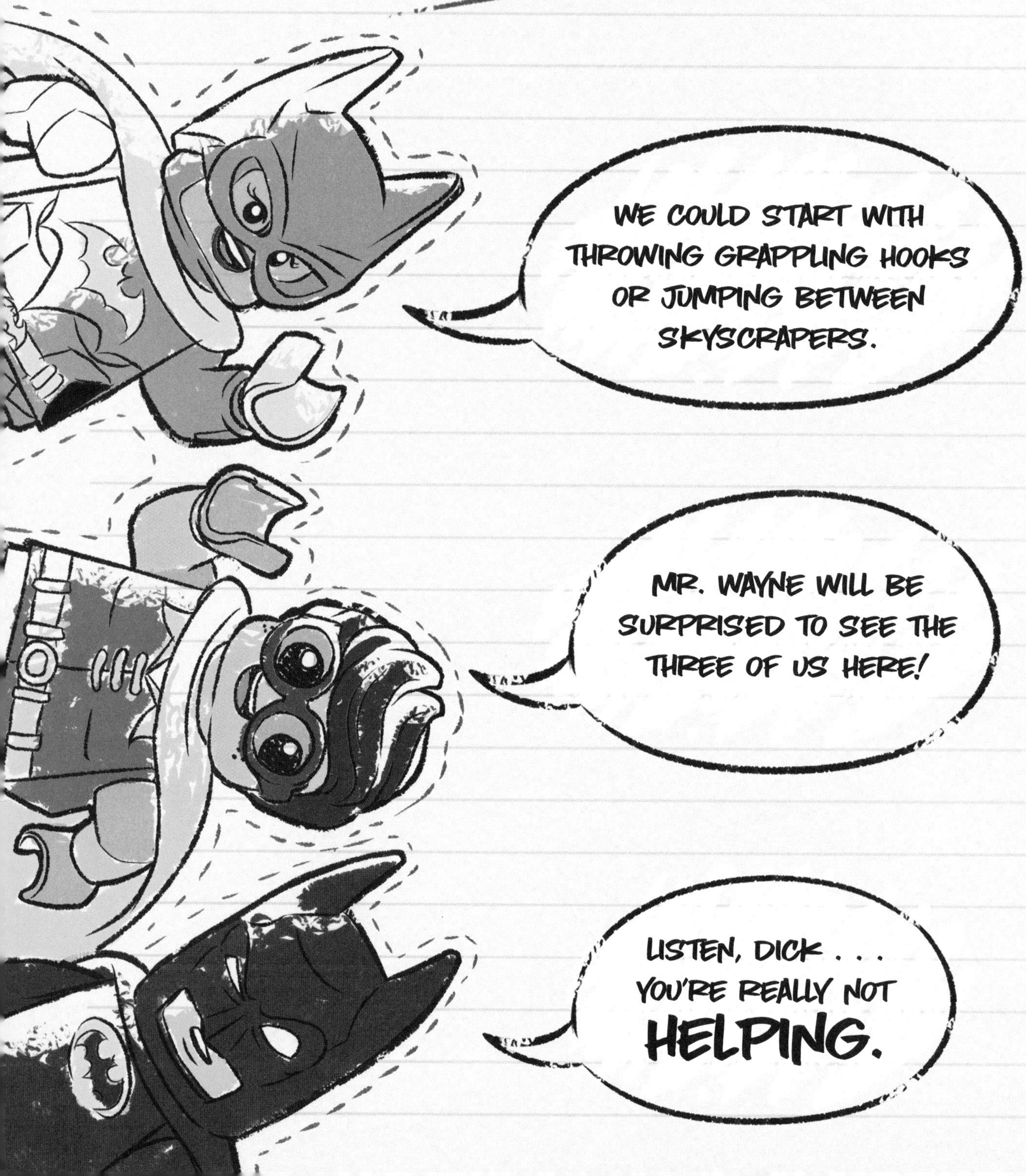
WE COULD START WITH THROWING GRAPPLING HOOKS OR JUMPING BETWEEN SKYSCRAPERS.
MR. WAYNE WILL BE SURPRISED TO SEE THE THREE OF US HERE!
LISTEN, DICK . . . YOU'RE REALLY NOT HELPING.

DRAW AND DESCRIBE SOME PHYSICAL EXERCISES FOR A SUPER HERO-IN-TRAINING:

DRAW SOME PICTURES OF ME TRAINING ROBIN HERE.

I CAN'T STOP THINKING ABOUT THAT

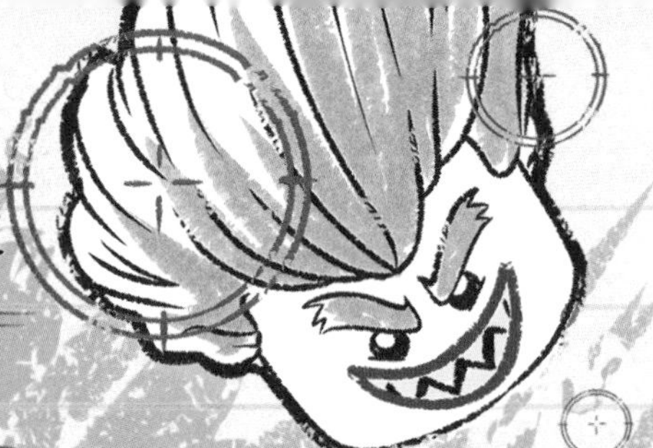

CLOWN

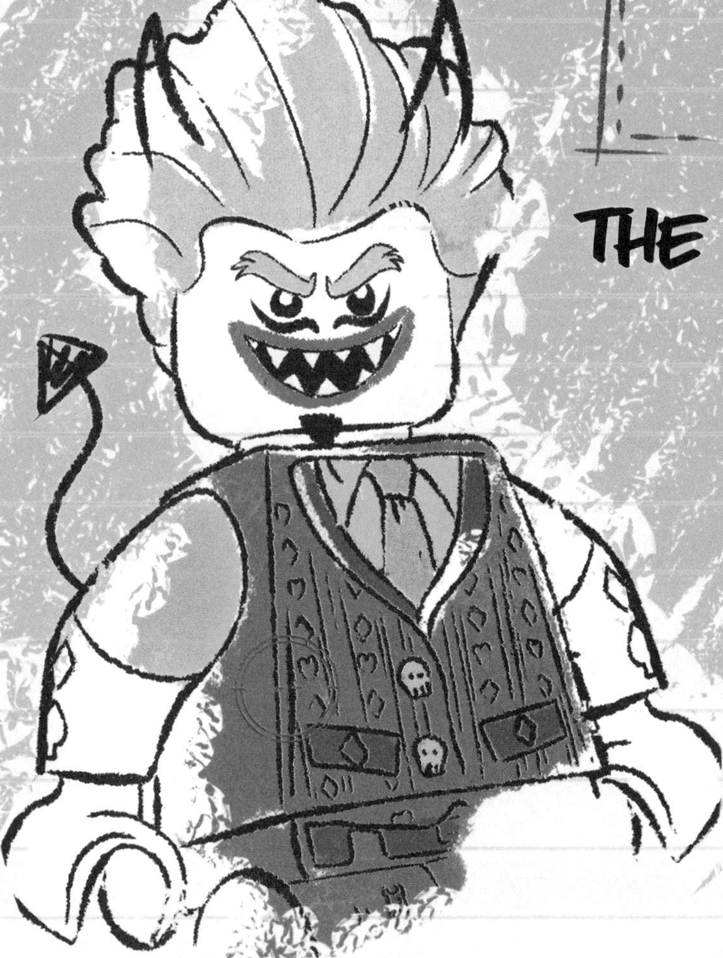

THE JOKER . . .

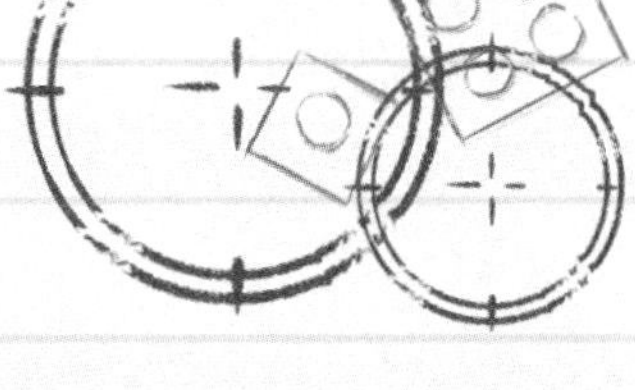

I NEED TO GET RID OF HIM

ONCE AND FOR ALL.

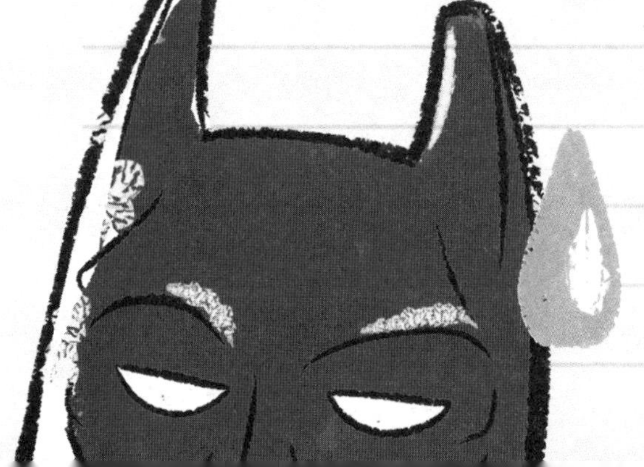

I JUST DON'T KNOW WHAT THE BEST WAY TO DO THAT IS YET.

COULD I SEND HIM UP TO THE MOON IN A ROCKET?

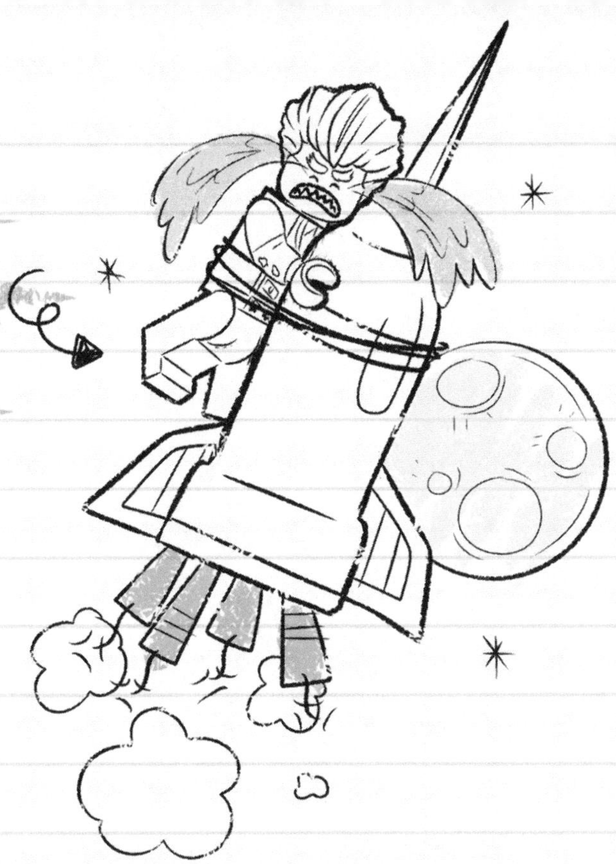

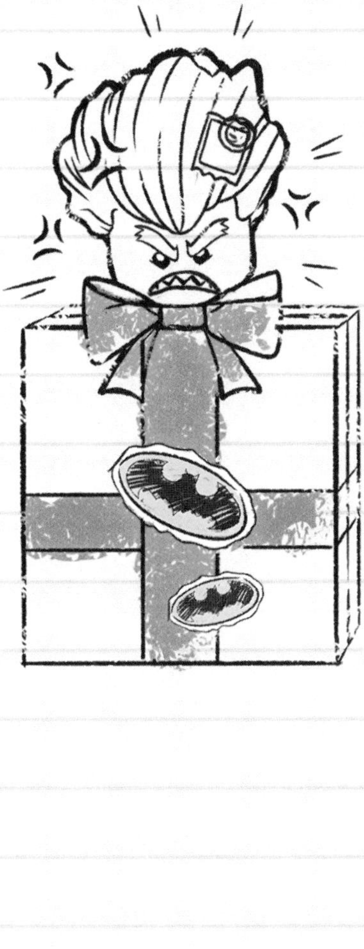

OR PACK HIM UP AND SHIP HIM TO A DESERTED ISLAND?

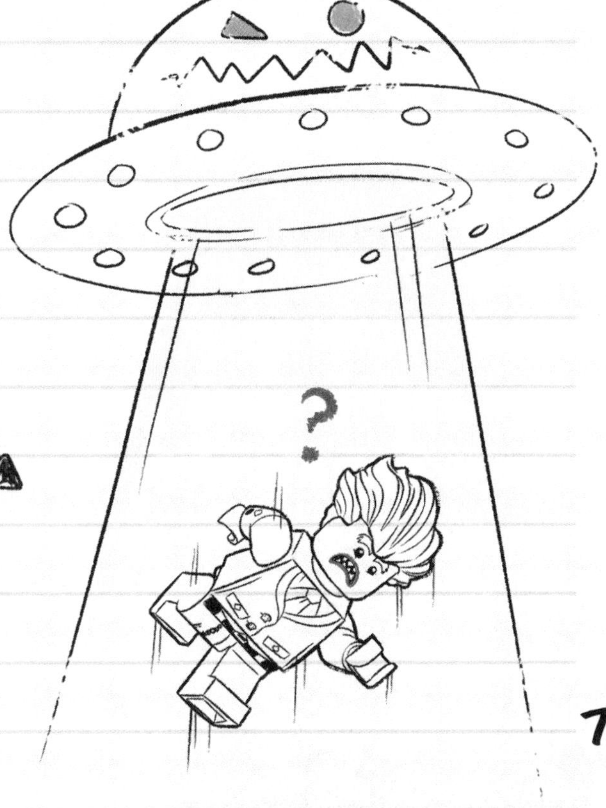

OR MAYBE I COULD ARRANGE FOR HIM TO BE **ABDUCTED BY ALIENS?**

Can you think of some other inventive ways to get rid of the JOKER?

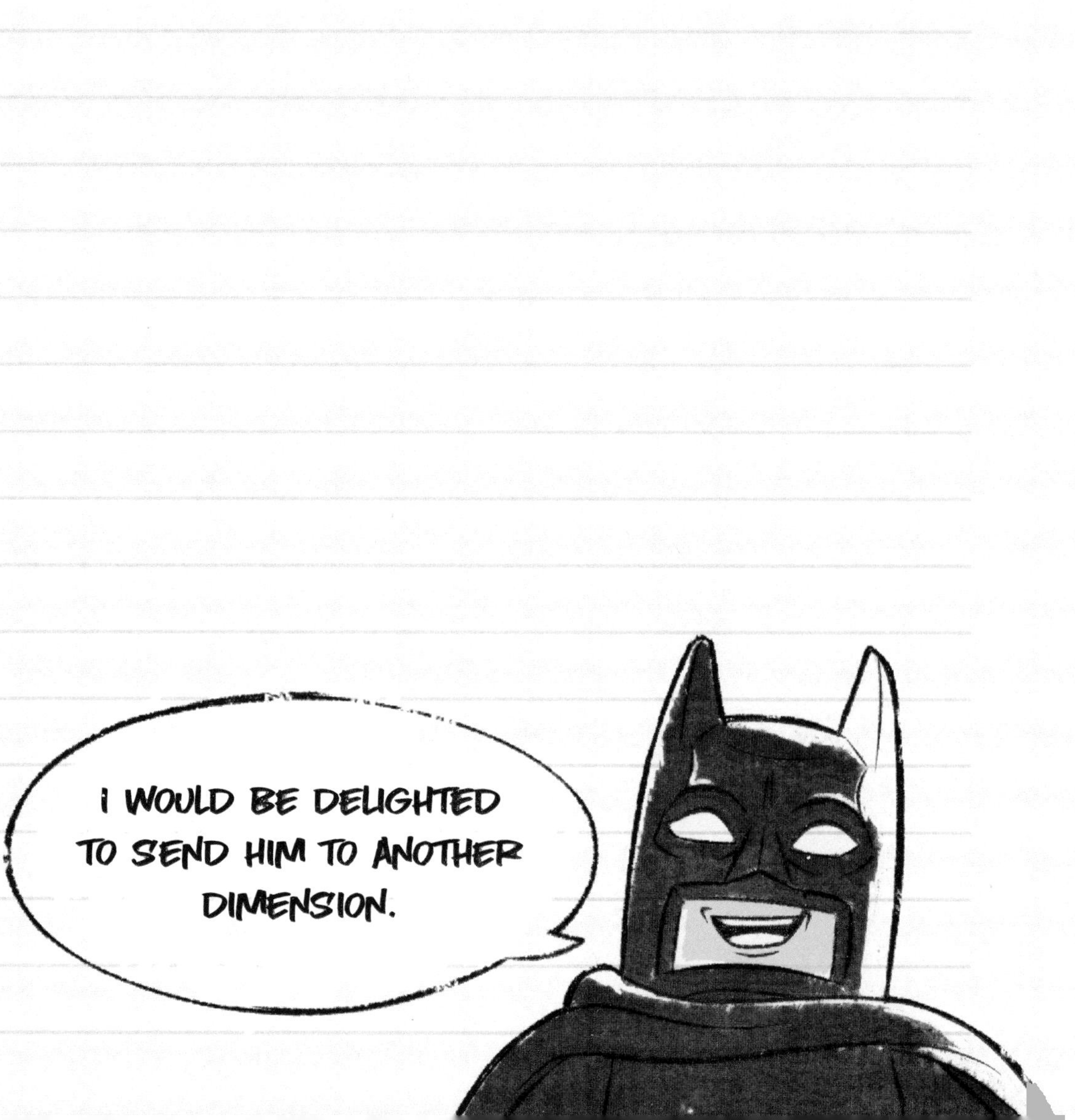
I WOULD BE DELIGHTED TO SEND HIM TO ANOTHER DIMENSION.

Something **PRETTY AWESOME** happened today.
Dick found an old sheet of paper in my desk . . .

Bruce Wayne, AGE 9

✓ A Super Hero

✓ Saves the world. Fights mighty super-villains with cosmic powers. (Ambitious but not impossible)

✓ Wears the coolest costume, preferably with a mask, armor, and the most awesome symbol ever!

✓ Has tons of gadgets . . . firing ropes, hooks, shurikens, exploding orbs, smoke grenades, night vision devices, winged capes that turn into paragliders!

✓ Defeats villains using kung fu, karate, judo, ninjutsu, jiu-jitsu, Brazilian jiu-jitsu, aikido, boxing, Thai boxing, tae kwon do, capoeira, kendo, kyudo. (I don't know any more martial arts but it would be good to have more than 127.)

✓ Owns huge battle machines that fly, float, ride, crush, shoot . . . all with amazing style and wow factor!

IT WAS **THE BEGINNING** OF MY PATH TO BECOMING BATMAN.

WHO SHOULD I BECOME IN THE FUTURE?

A **SUPER HERO** OR A **BILLIONAIRE** BUSINESSMAN?

A BILLIONAIRE BUSINESSMAN

- EARNS MONEY AND LIVES COMFORTABLY. (NOT SURE HOW TO LIVE COMFORTABLY IF I NEED TO EARN MONEY ALL THE TIME?)
- WEARS A SUIT, A PAIR OF SNEAKERS, AND ALL THE LATEST TRENDS TO THE MANAGEMENT BOARD MEETINGS.
- HAS AN ELEGANT NOTEBOOK AND COMPUTER. (WITH AT LEAST 100 GAMES, IN CASE I'M "BORED" AT THE "BOARD" MEETINGS . . . GET IT?)
- GOES TO WEEKLY MANAGEMENT BOARD MEETINGS. (I NEED TO FIND OUT WHAT THIS "BOARD" ACTUALLY IS, BUT I'M PRETTY SURE IT'S NOT RELATED TO A SKATEBOARD, WHICH IS A SHAME.)
- OWNS A FANCY LIMO, YACHT, MAYBE A JET SKATEBOARD FOR THE YACHT (OR FOR THE BOARD MEETINGS).

HEY, WHY NOT BOTH! :D

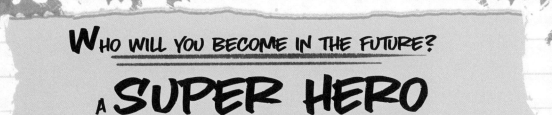

Who will you become in the future?
A SUPER HERO
or something else entirely?

DRAW AND DESCRIBE YOUR FUTURE SELF HERE.

I AM BATMAN AND I AM . . . OUT OF SPACE IN THE
JOURNAL SECTION. MAYBE IT'S A SIGN FOR ME TO
LEAP INTO ACTION! ALL RIGHT, MY AWESOME FANS,
BATMAN IS PUTTING DOWN HIS PEN.

LET'S DO SOME STICKER ACTIVITIES!

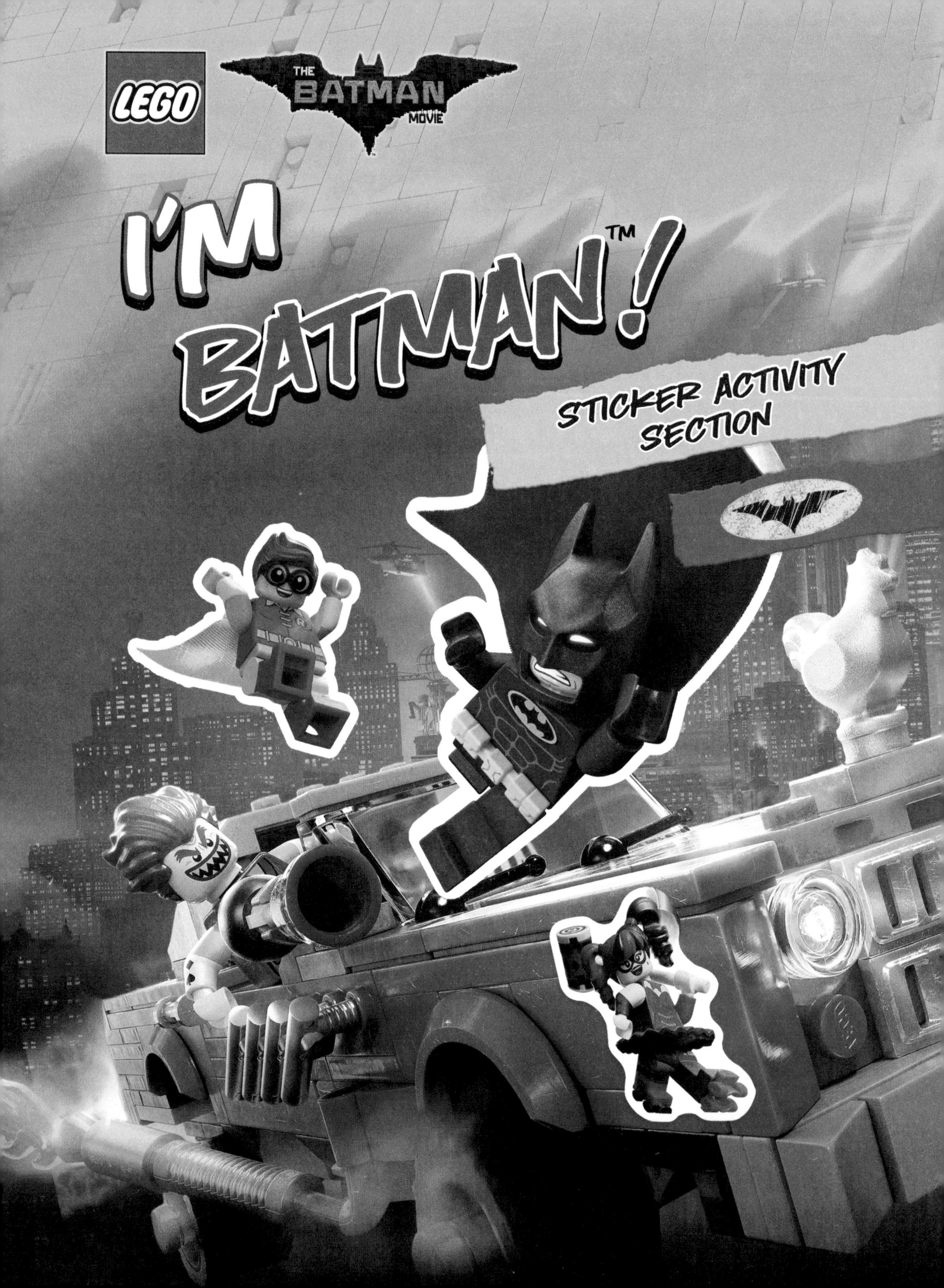
LEGO
THE BATMAN MOVIE
I'M BATMAN!™
STICKER ACTIVITY SECTION

WELCOME TO WAYNE MANOR

SOMEWHERE ON THE OUTSKIRTS OF GOTHAM CITY, QUITE CLOSE TO ARKHAM ASYLUM, THERE'S A GIANT MANSION CALLED WAYNE MANOR. IT IS BUILT FROM THOUSANDS OF BRICKS AND PROTECTS THE SECRETS OF THOSE WHO LIVE THERE.

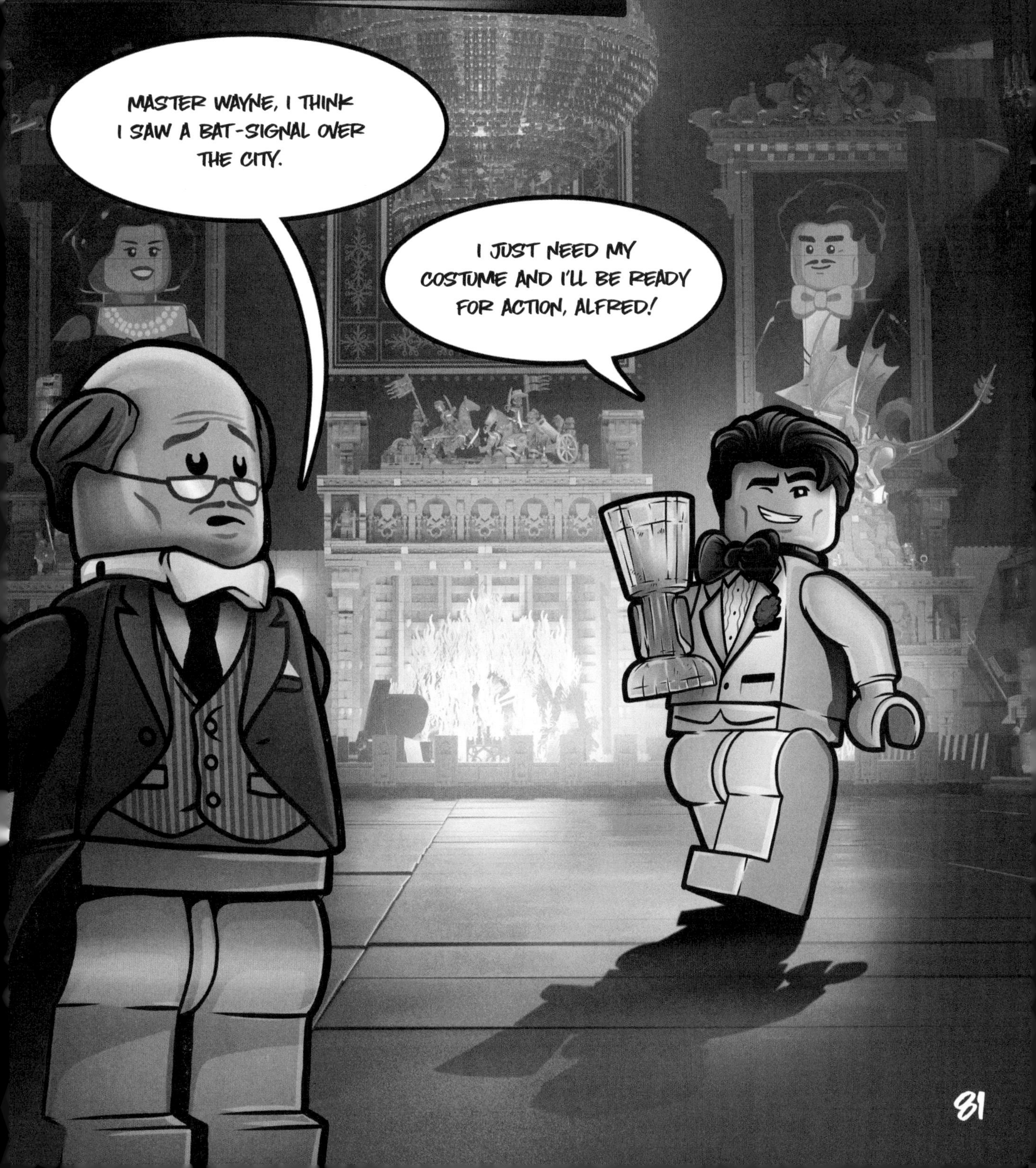
MASTER WAYNE, I THINK I SAW A BAT-SIGNAL OVER THE CITY.
I JUST NEED MY COSTUME AND I'LL BE READY FOR ACTION, ALFRED!

ESCAPE FROM ARKHAM

THE JOKER AND HARLEY QUINN ARE ESCAPING FROM ARKHAM ASYLUM! ARE THEY TRYING TO TAKE OVER GOTHAM CITY ON THEIR OWN? FIND THE REST OF THEIR VILLAINOUS GANG AND ADD THEM TO THE PAGE.

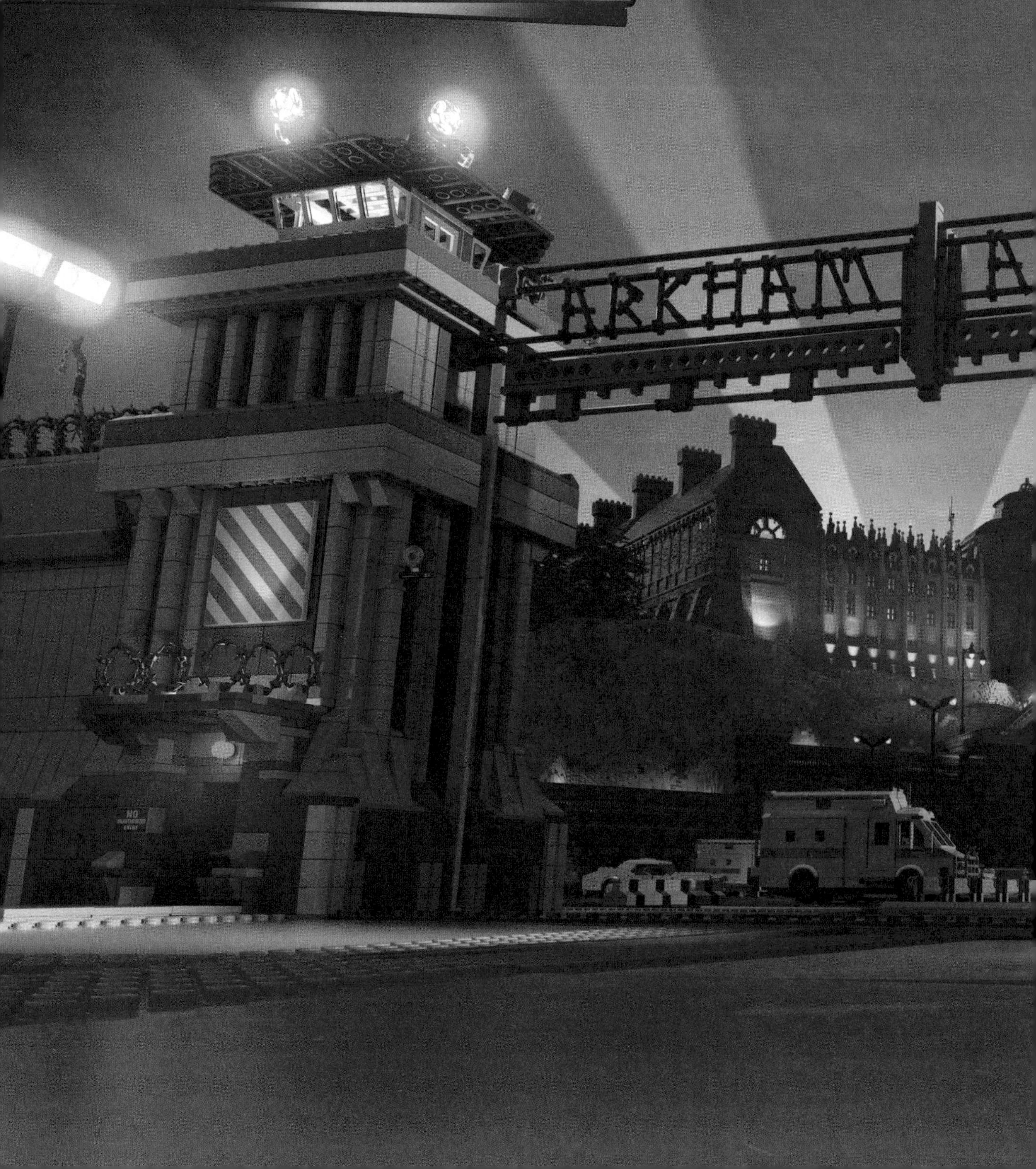
ARKHAM A
NO

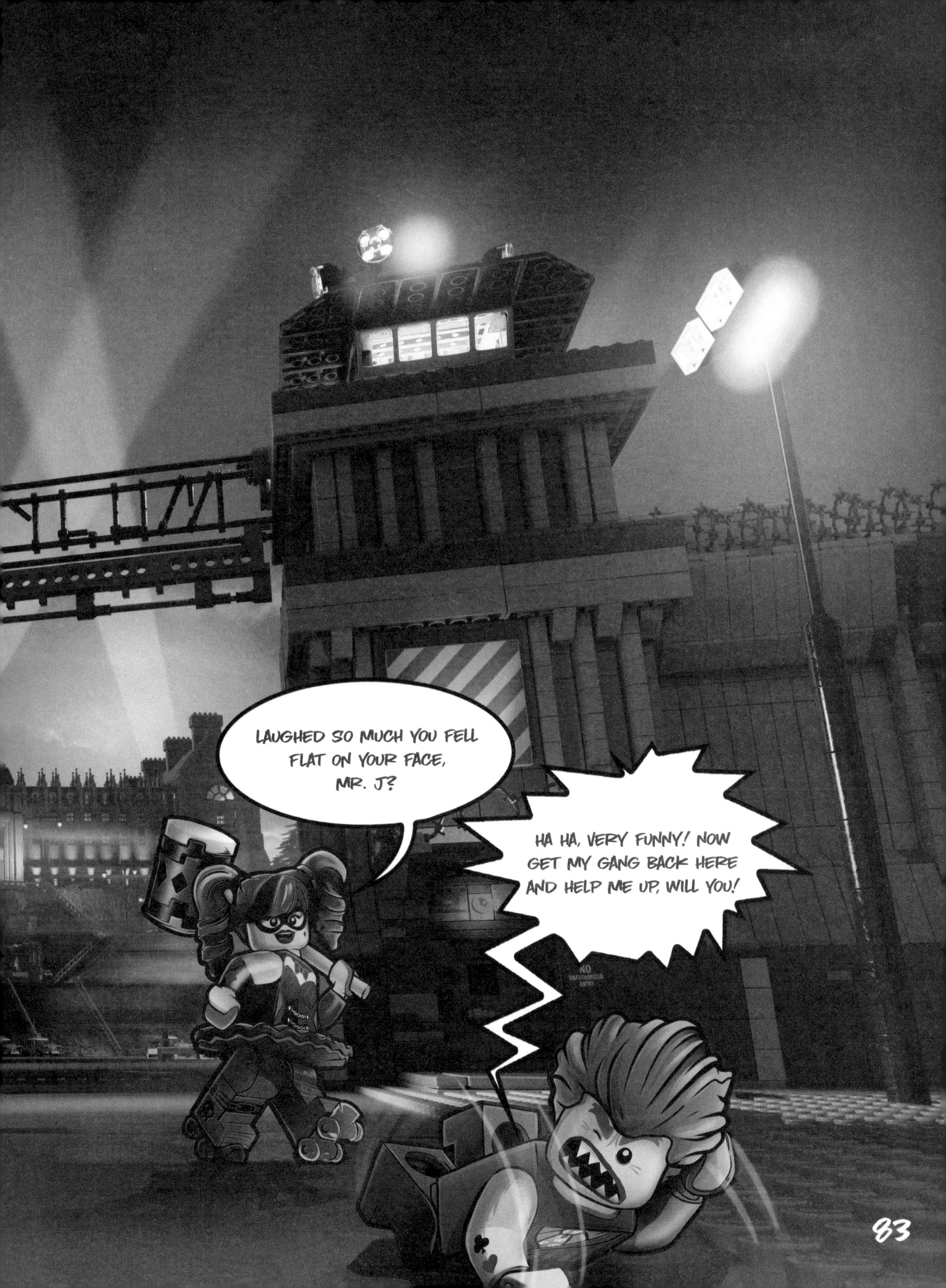
LAUGHED SO MUCH YOU FELL FLAT ON YOUR FACE, MR. J?
HA HA, VERY FUNNY! NOW GET MY GANG BACK HERE AND HELP ME UP, WILL YOU!

SCUTTLER COUNTERATTACKS

USE YOUR STICKERS TO PREPARE THE GIANT SCUTTLER FOR ACTION. THEN ADD SOME CREATURES FLYING AROUND THE BATCAVE.

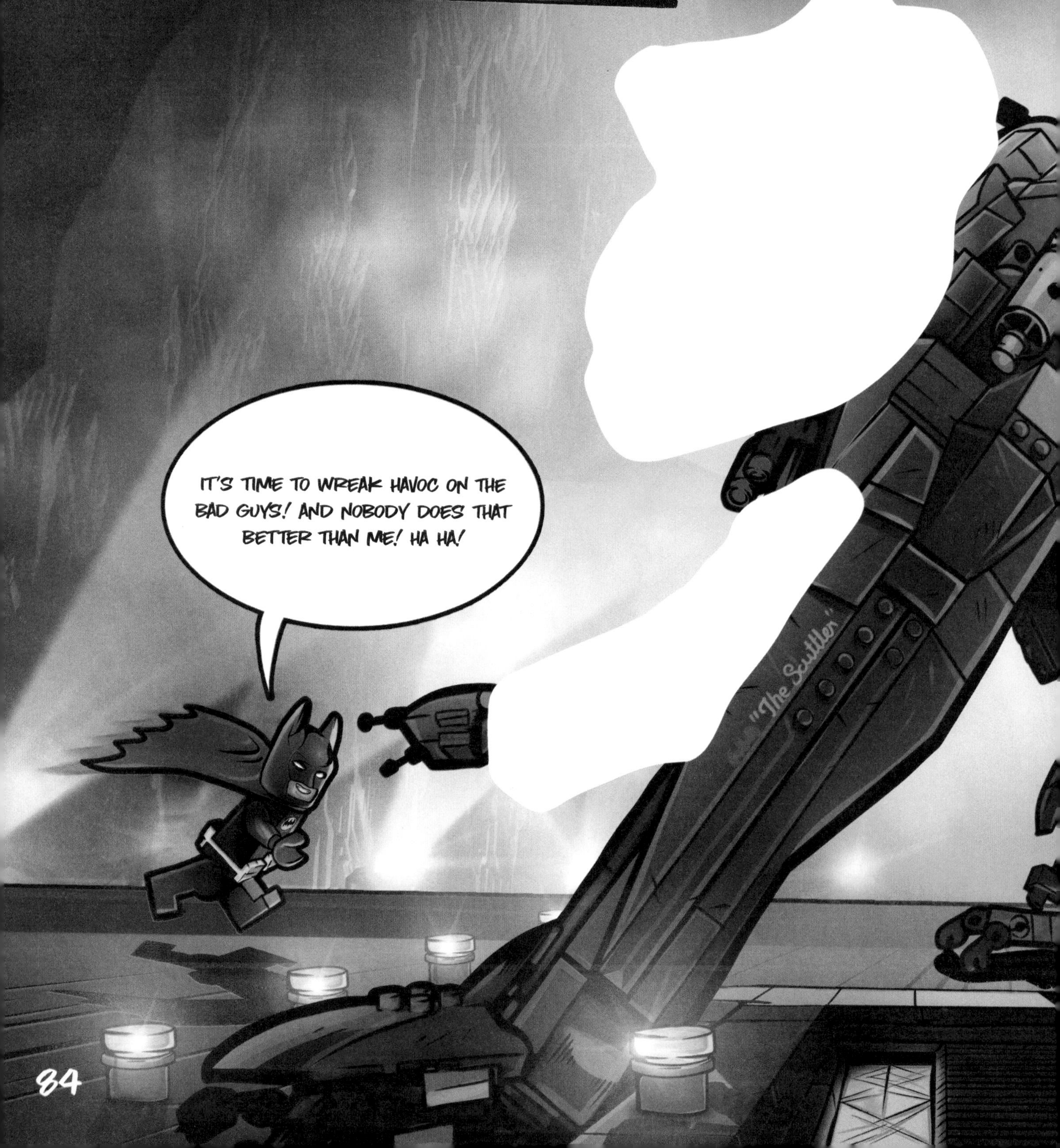
IT'S TIME TO WREAK HAVOC ON THE BAD GUYS! AND NOBODY DOES THAT BETTER THAN ME! HA HA!
"The Scuttler"

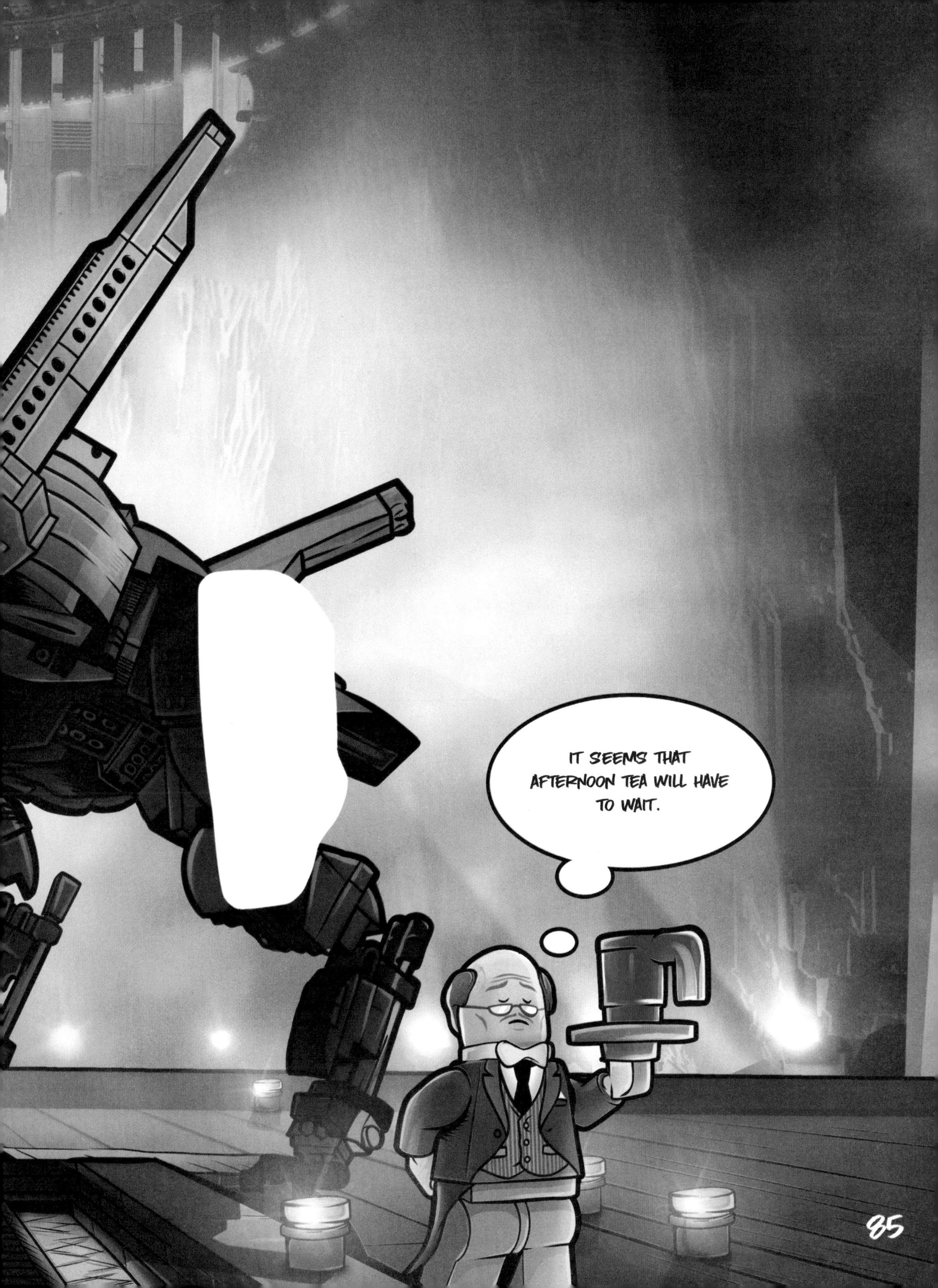
IT SEEMS THAT AFTERNOON TEA WILL HAVE TO WAIT.

HELP IS ON THE WAY!

COMMISSIONER GORDON OFFERS BATMAN SOME HELP. WHAT VILLAIN IS BATMAN GOING TO CONFRONT? STICK IN THE VILLAIN HE IS THINKING ABOUT.

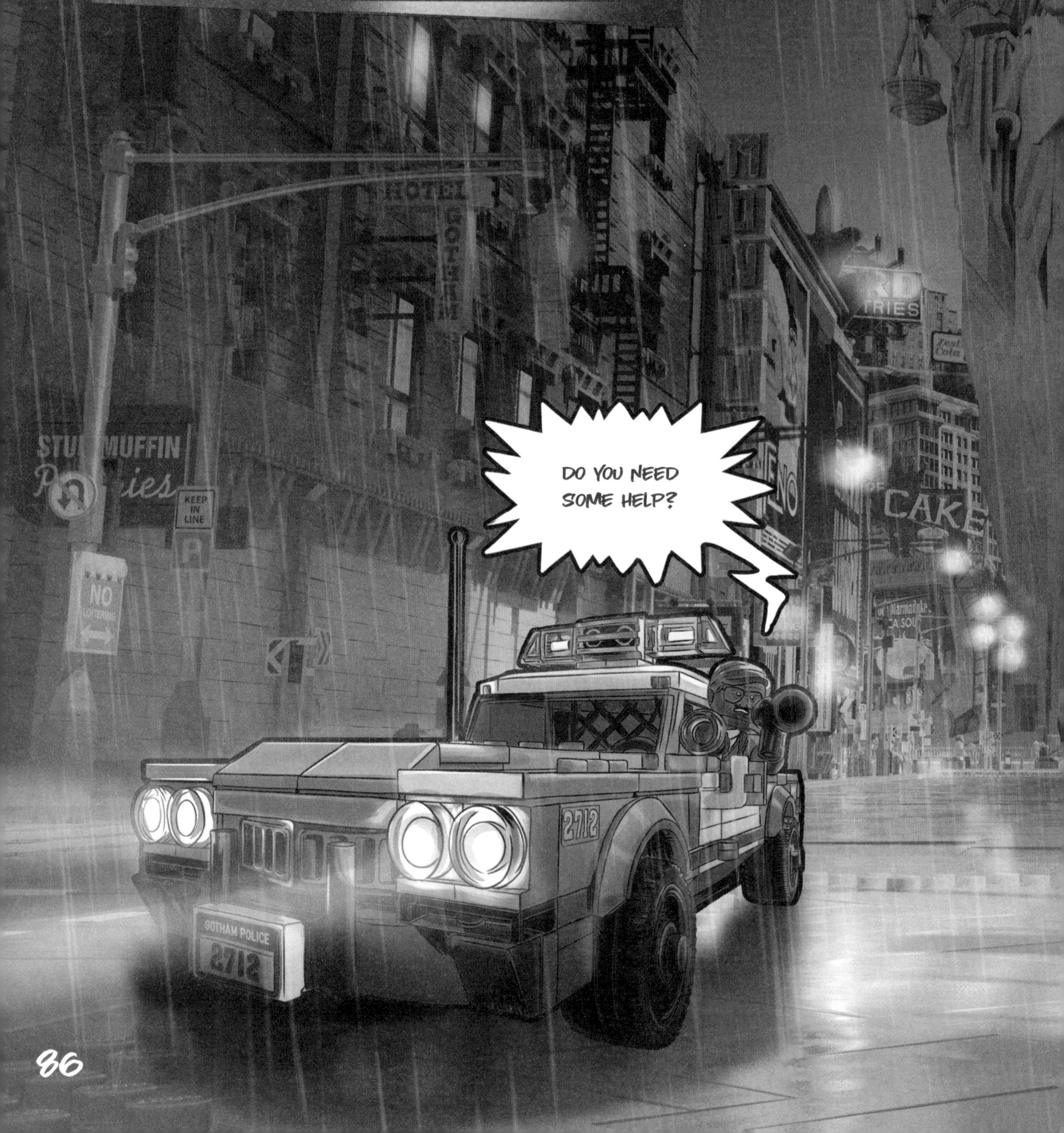

DO YOU NEED SOME HELP?
HOTEL
KEEP IN LINE
NO LOITERING
CAKE
2712
GOTHAM POLICE
2712

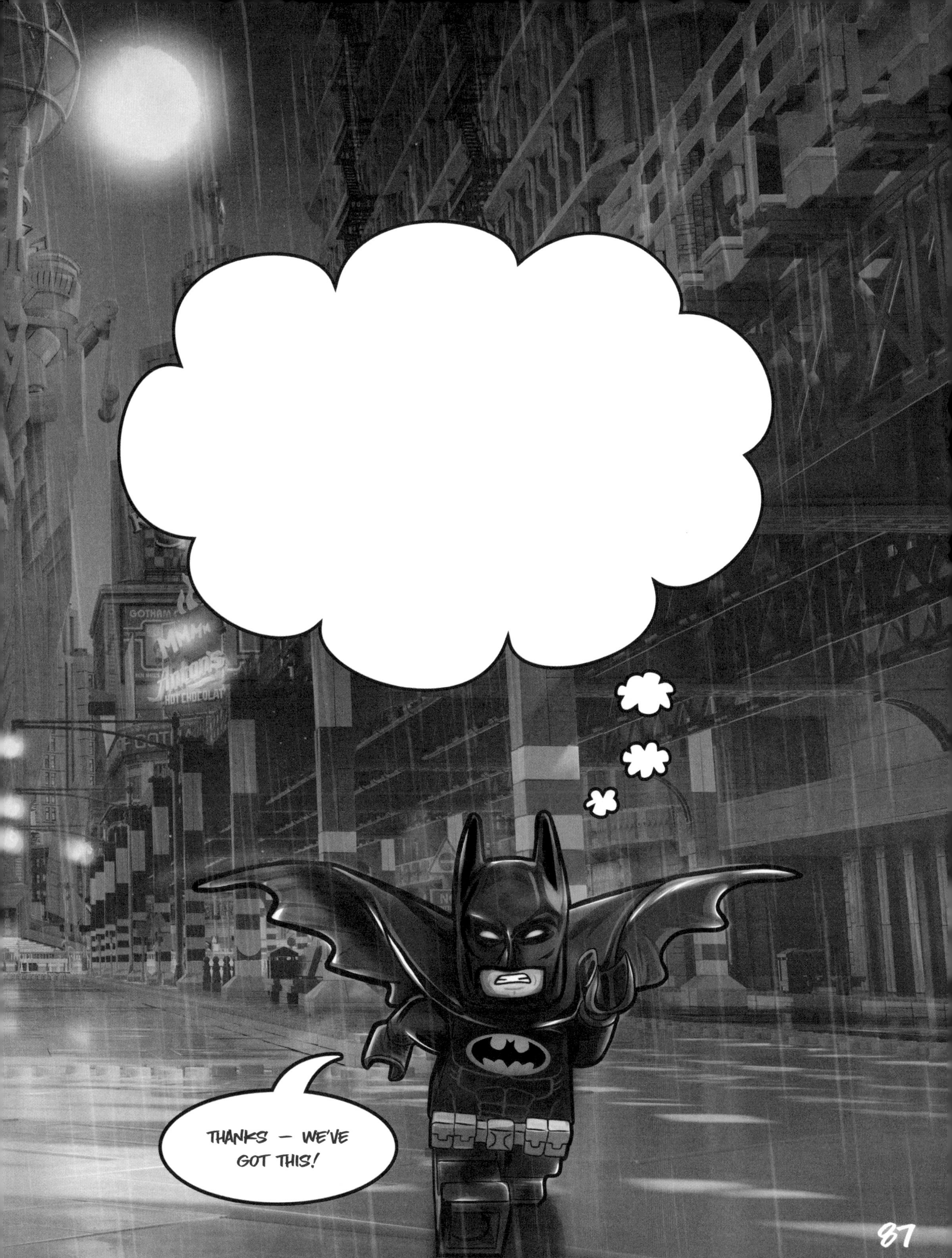
THANKS — WE'VE GOT THIS!

A DUEL WITH CLAYFACE

CLAYFACE IS A GIANT CLAY BEAST WHO DOESN'T LIKE BATMAN VERY MUCH. COMPLETE THE GIANT'S BODY WITH YOUR STICKERS SO THE DARK KNIGHT KNOWS WHERE TO STRIKE!

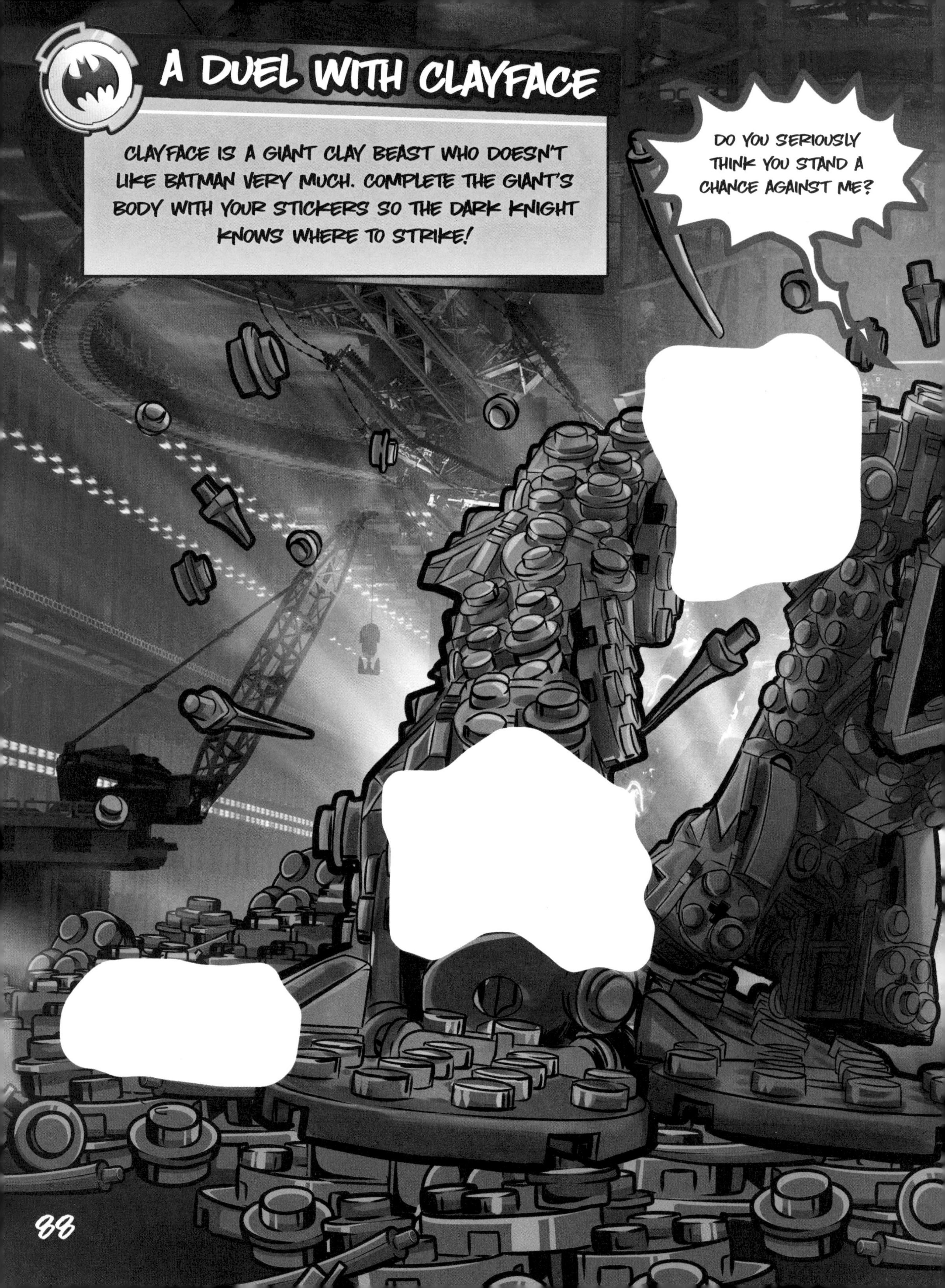
DO YOU SERIOUSLY THINK YOU STAND A CHANCE AGAINST ME?

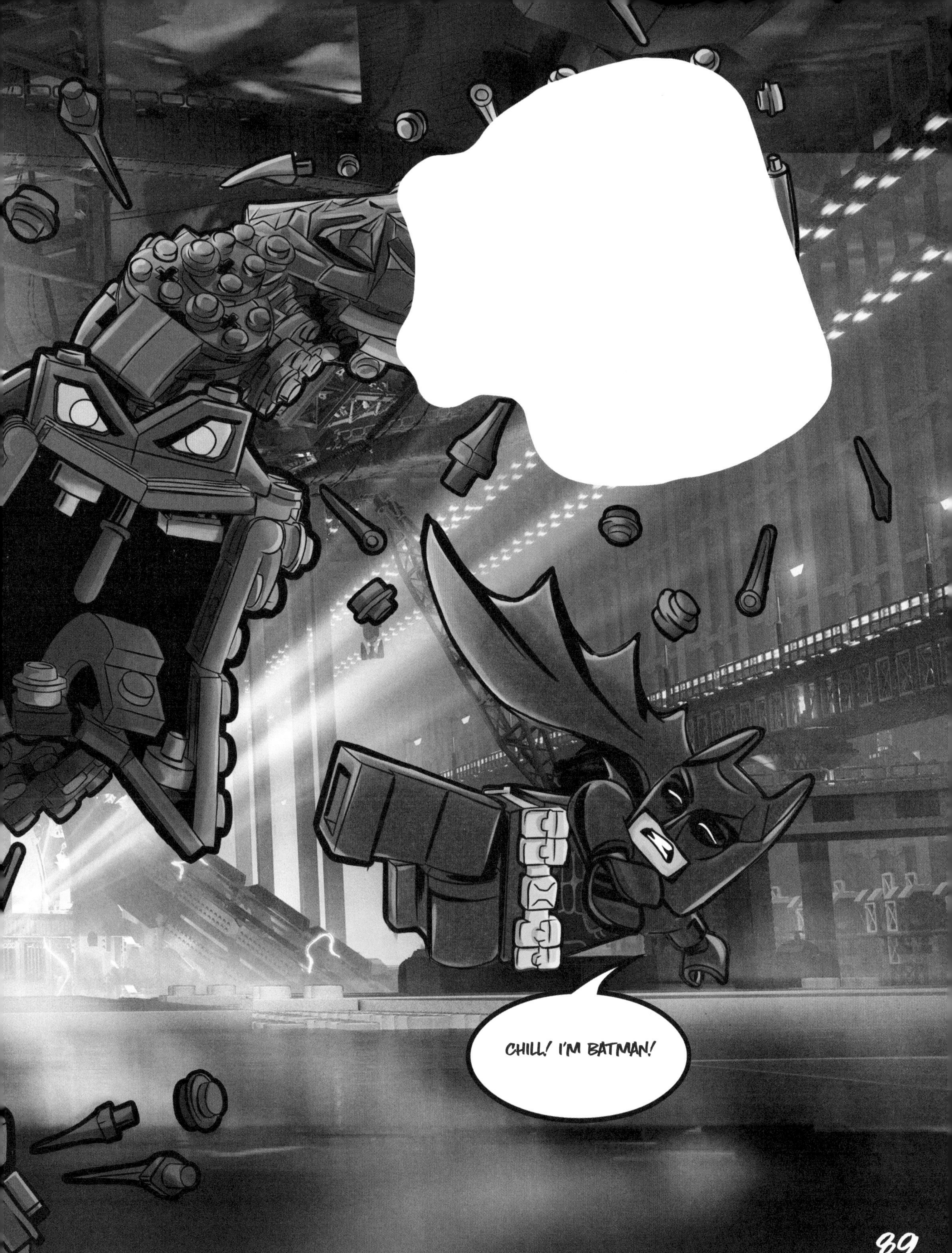
CHILL! I'M BATMAN!

A POISONOUS LABYRINTH

POISON IVY IS HIDING IN A MAZE OF VINES, BUT SHE'S NOT ALONE. LOOK AT THE SHADOWS AND USE YOUR STICKERS TO REVEAL WHO ELSE IS HIDING FROM BATMAN. THEN SHOW THE DARK KNIGHT THE WAY THROUGH.

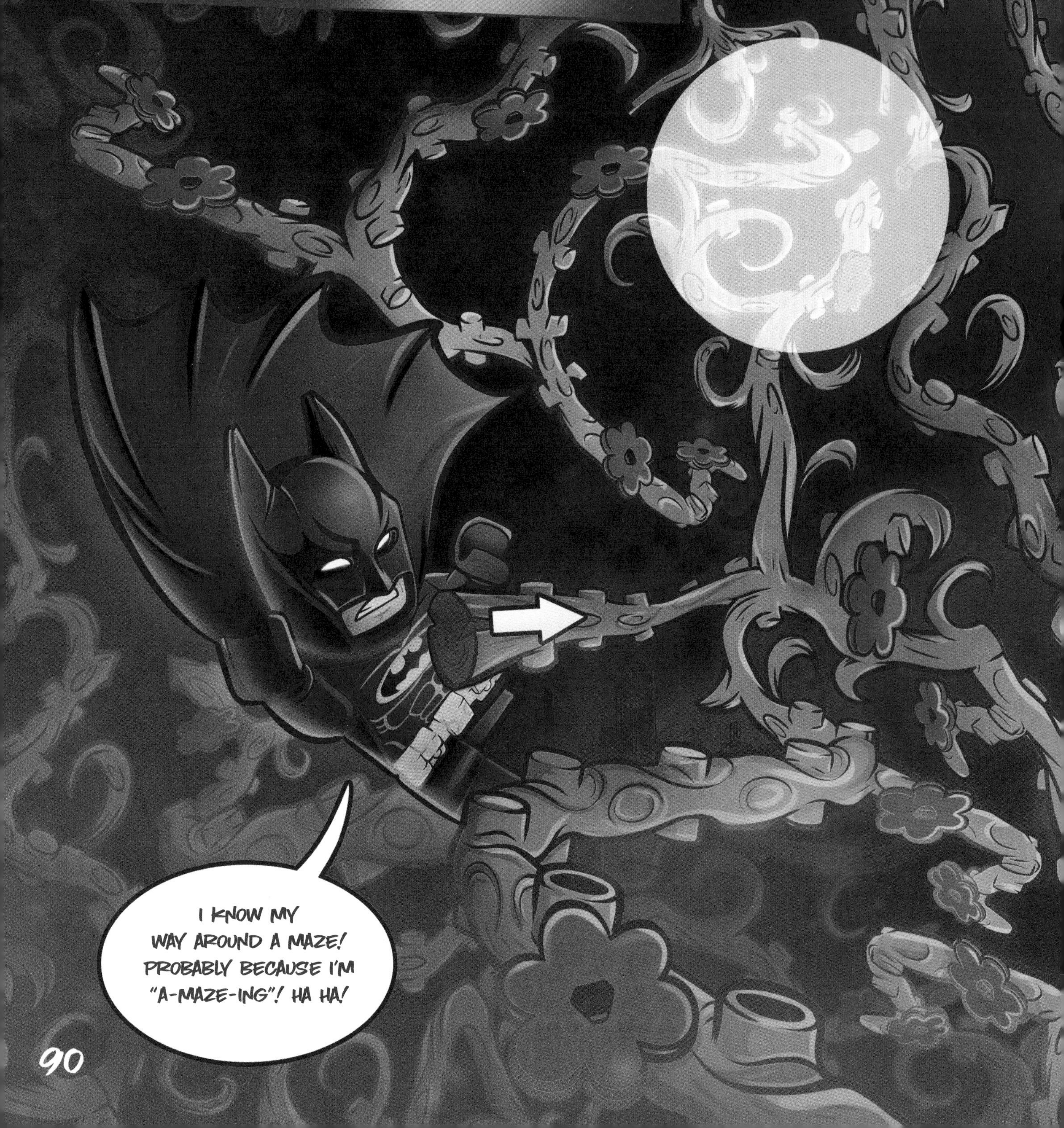
I KNOW MY WAY AROUND A MAZE! PROBABLY BECAUSE I'M "A-MAZE-ING"! HA HA!

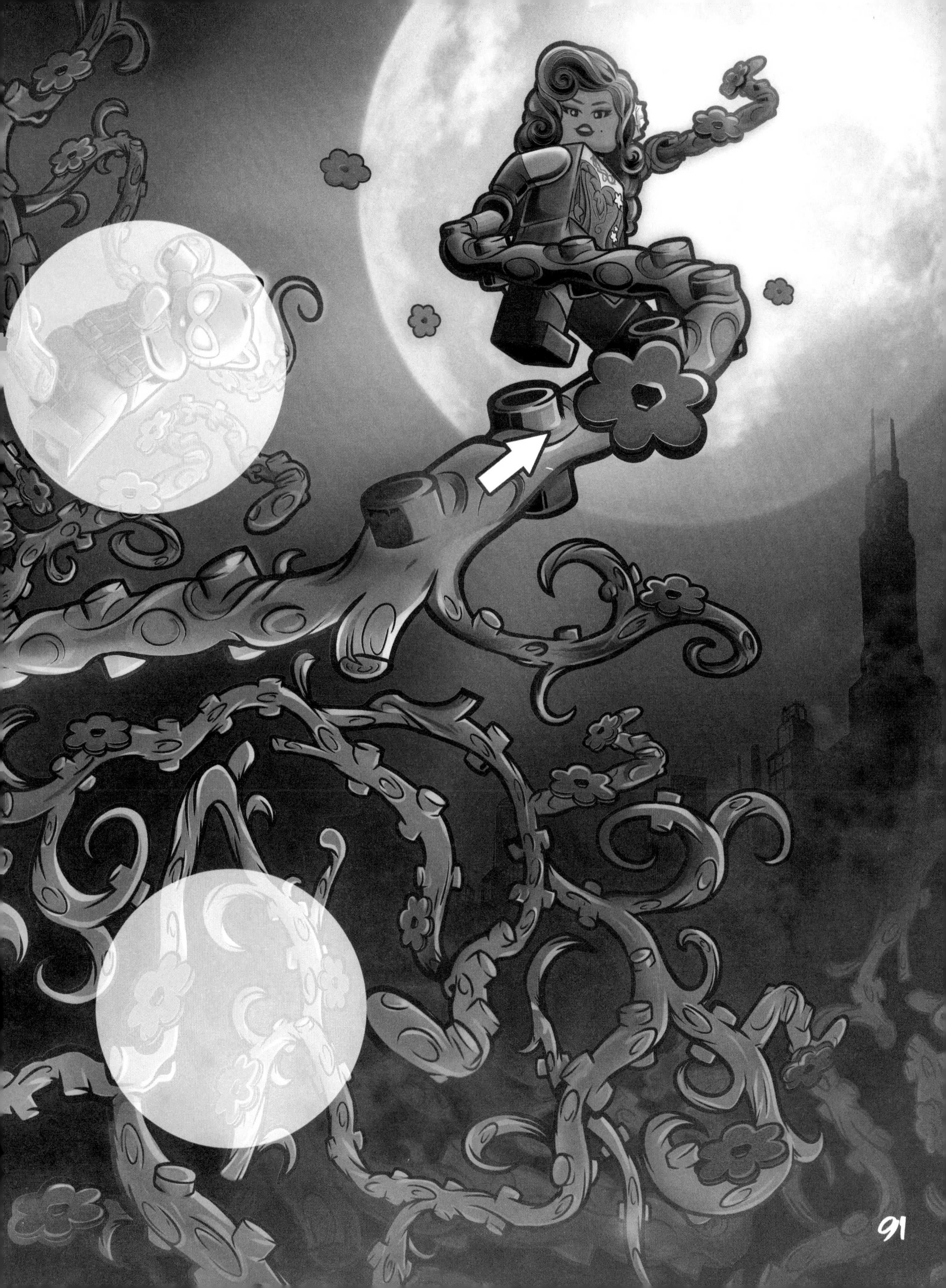

NIGHTTIME SURFING

THIS HUGE MACHINE CAN DO SO MUCH! RACING THROUGH THE CITY ON THE BATMOBILE AT FULL SPEED? EASY-PEASY . . . IT'S BATMAN'S VEHICLE AFTER ALL! COMPLETE THE BATMOBILE WITH YOUR STICKERS TO MAKE SURE IT HAS A SOFT LANDING.

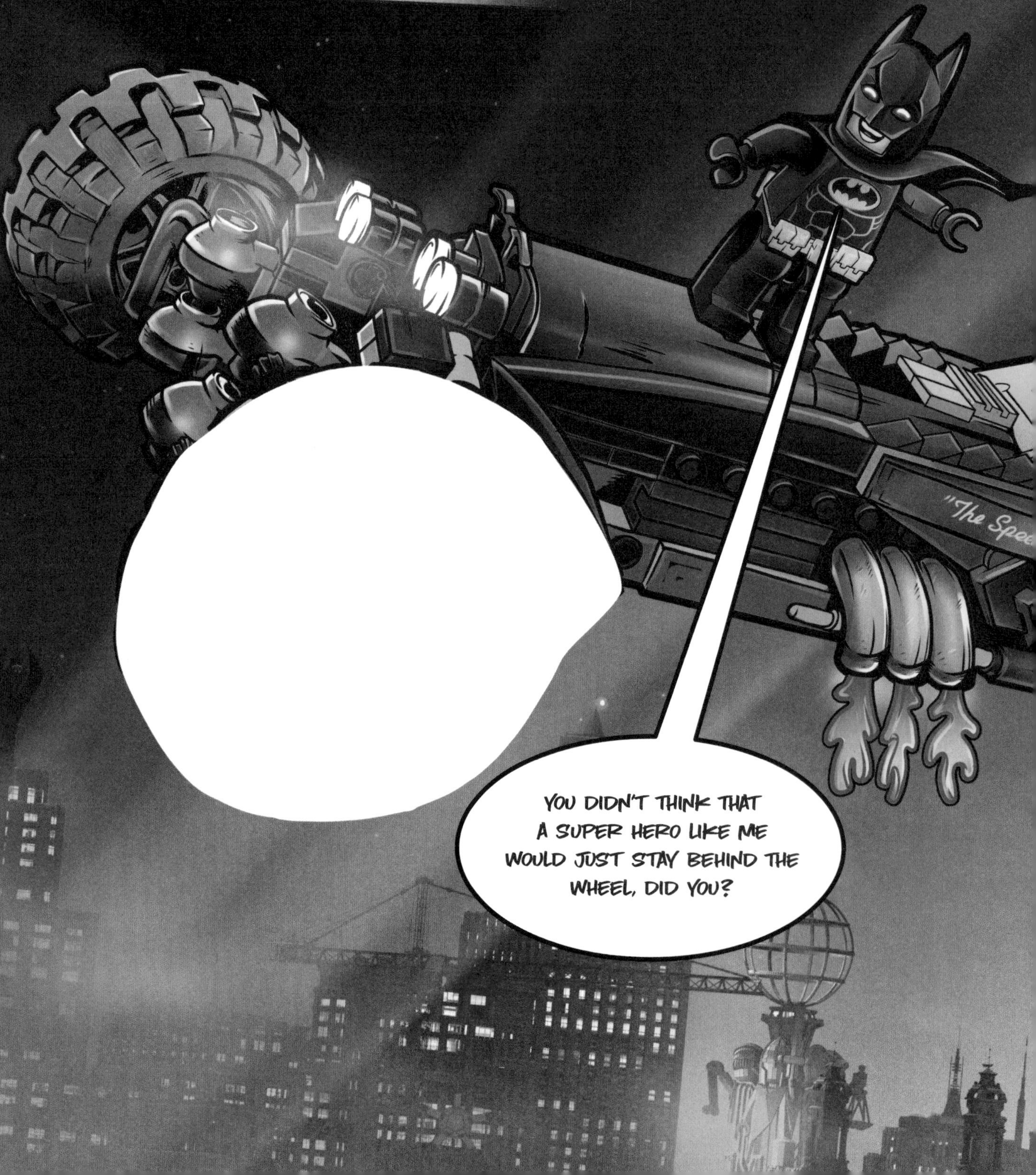
YOU DIDN'T THINK THAT A SUPER HERO LIKE ME WOULD JUST STAY BEHIND THE WHEEL, DID YOU?

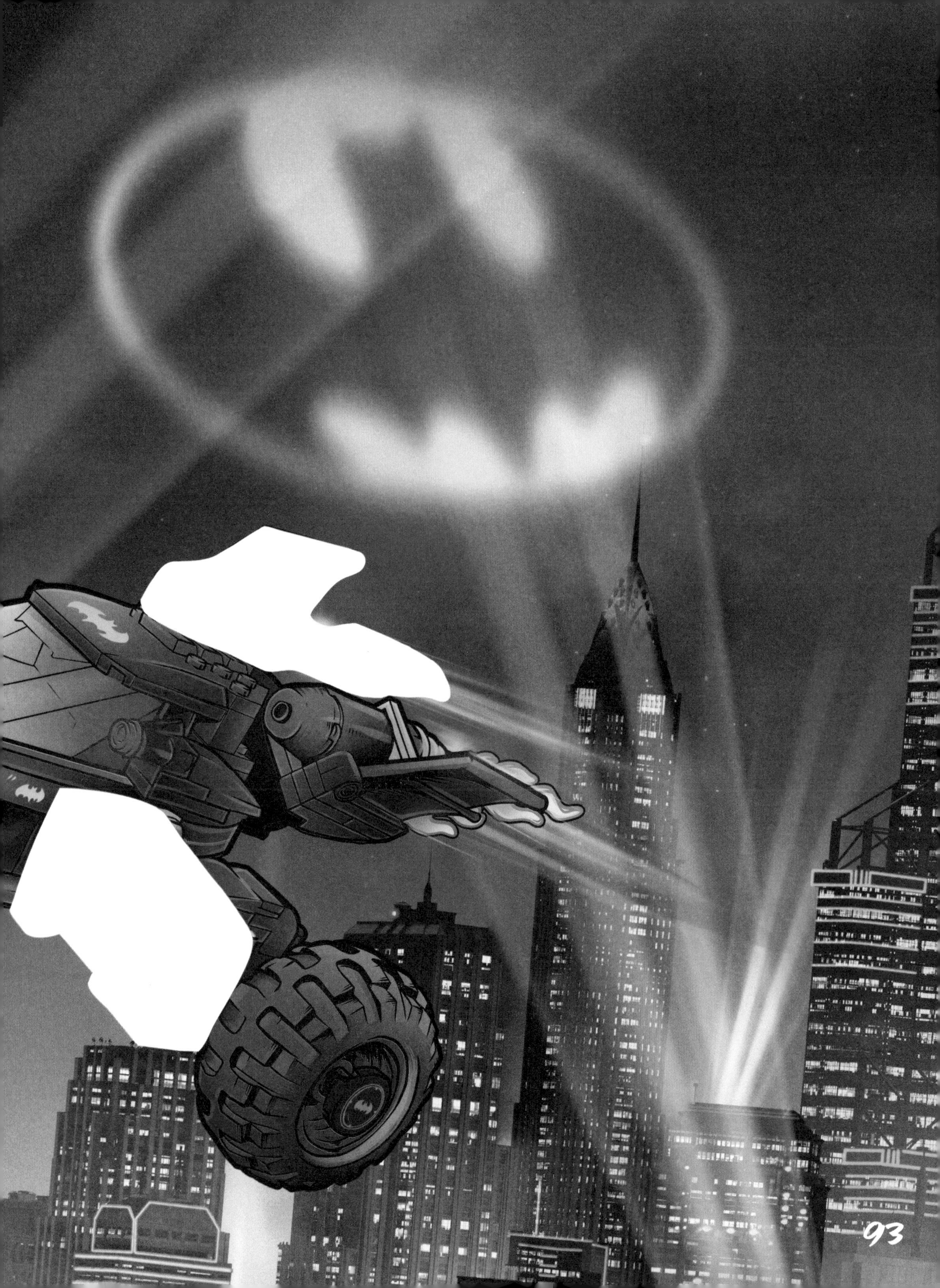

BANE'S ATTACK

WHO IS COMMISSIONER GORDON LOOKING FOR?
SEE IF YOU CAN FIND HIM!

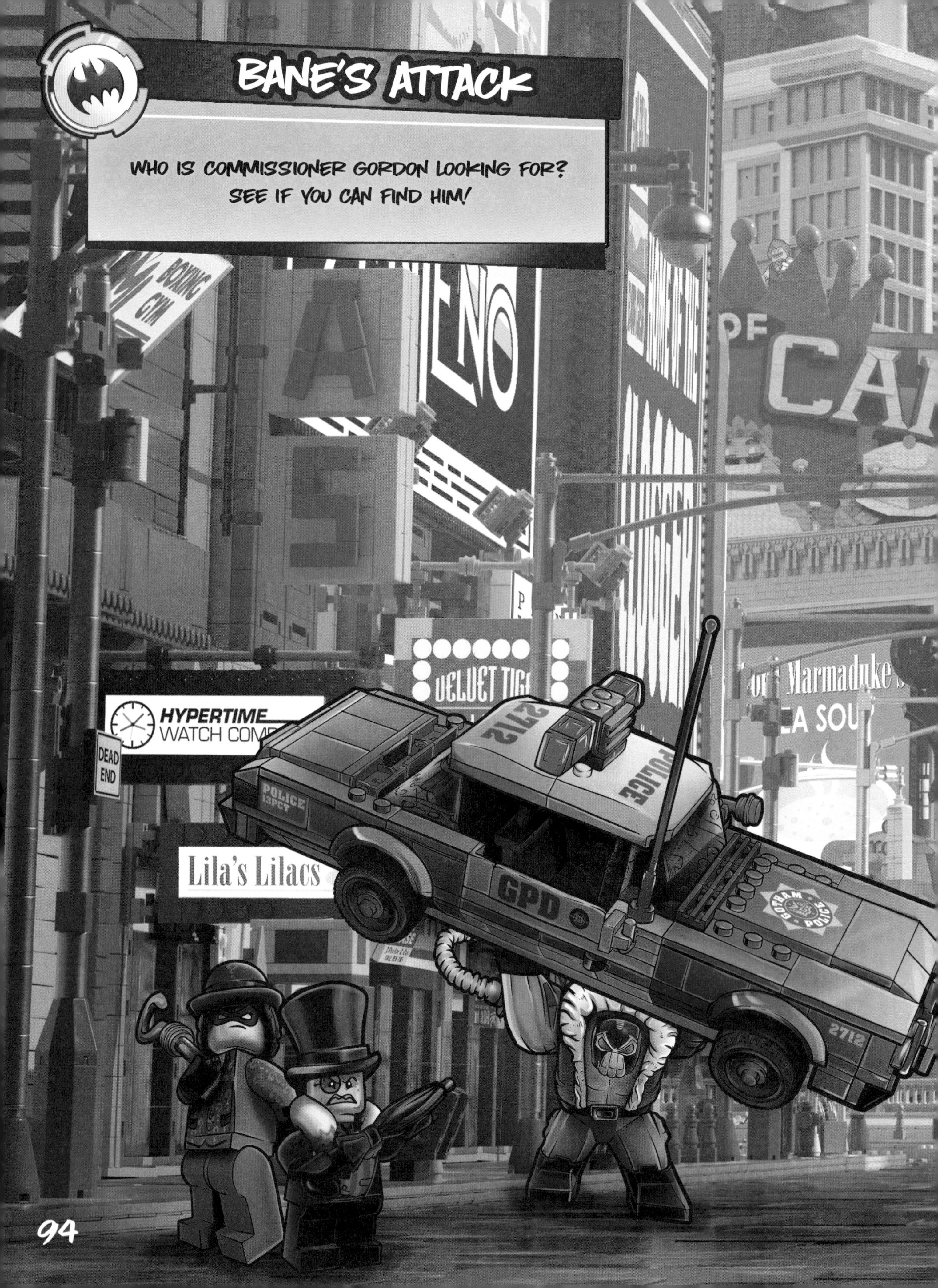
BOXING GYM
HYPERTIME WATCH COMP
DEAD END
Lila's Lilacs
Marmaduke's
POLICE
2712
GPD
GOTHAM POLICE

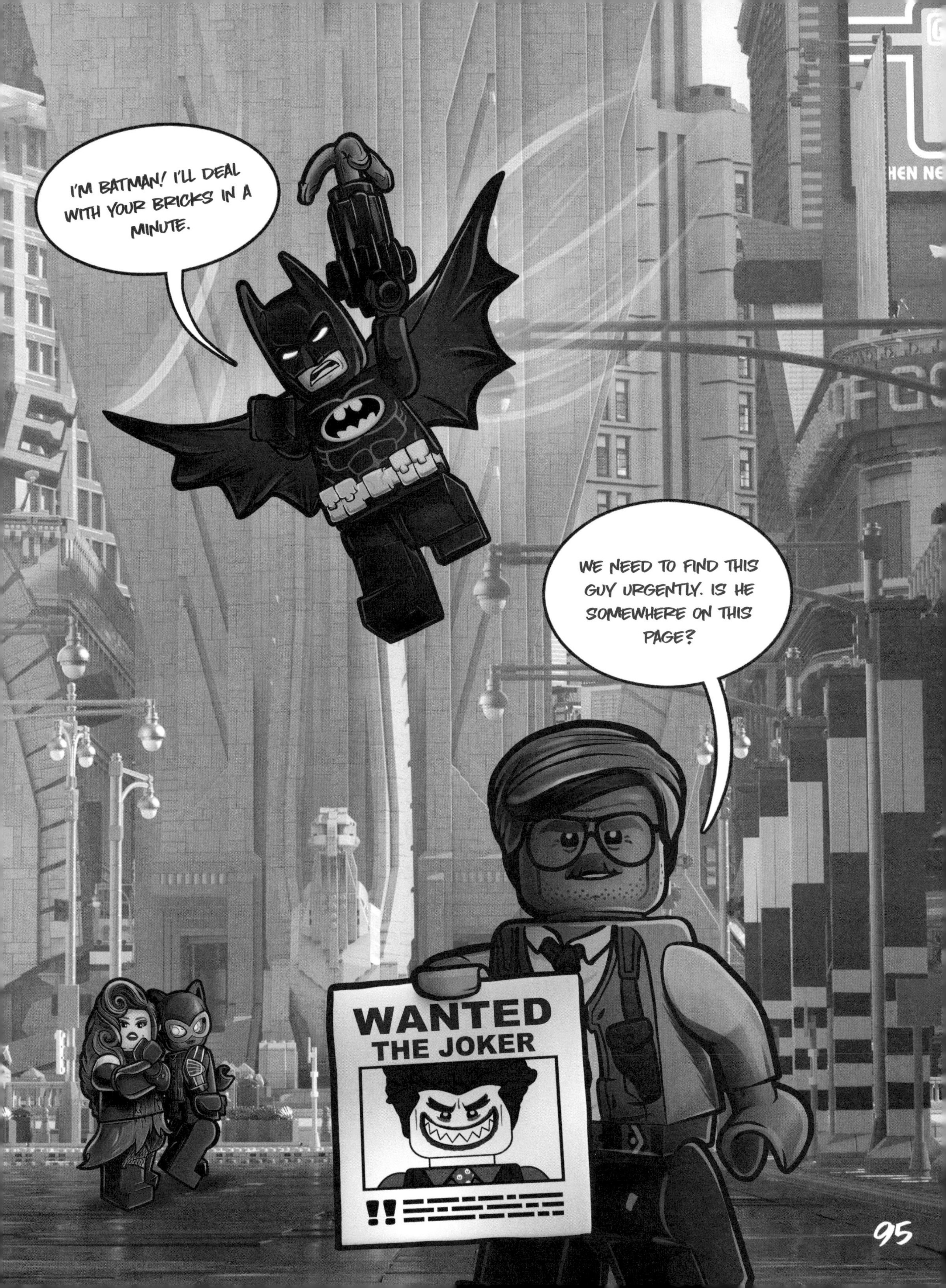
I'M BATMAN! I'LL DEAL WITH YOUR BRICKS IN A MINUTE.
WE NEED TO FIND THIS GUY URGENTLY. IS HE SOMEWHERE ON THIS PAGE?
WANTED
THE JOKER

ANSWERS

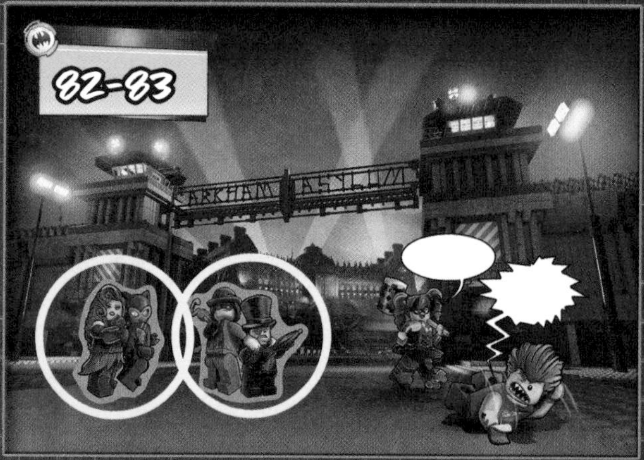
82-83
ARKHAM ASYLUM

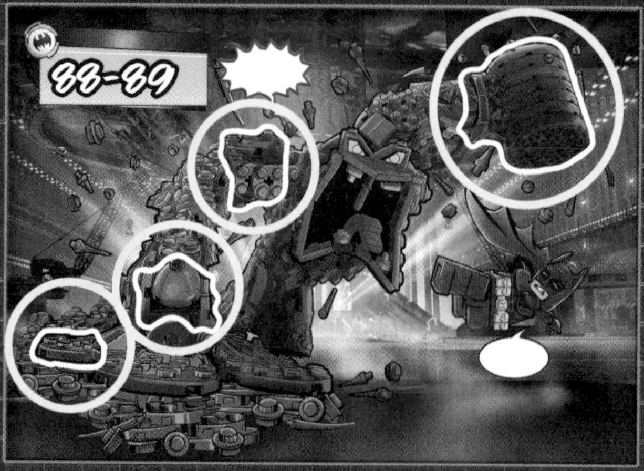
88-89

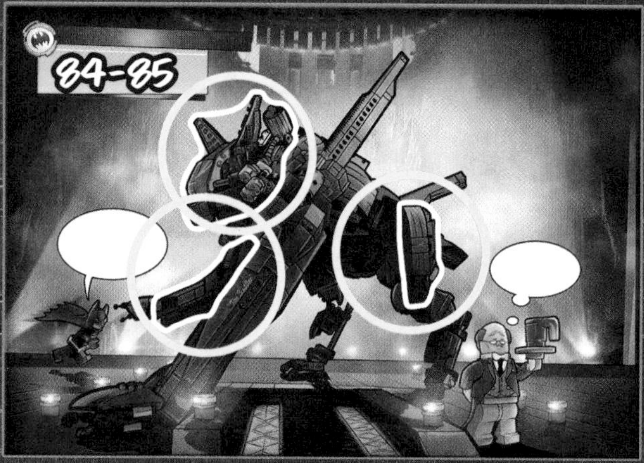
84-85

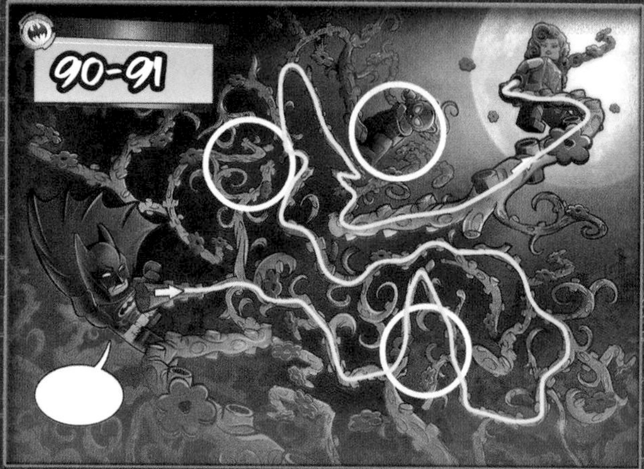
90-91

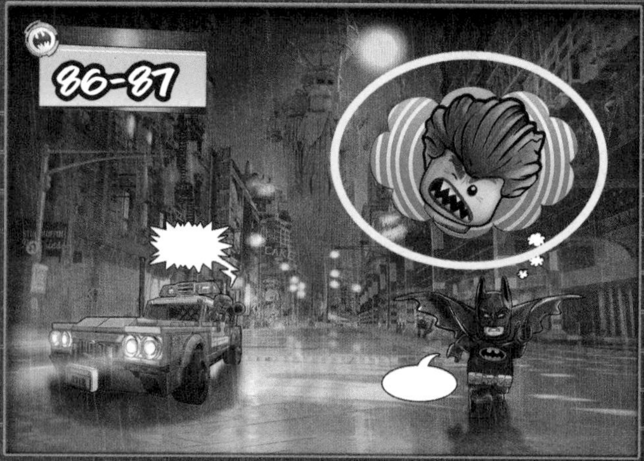
86-87

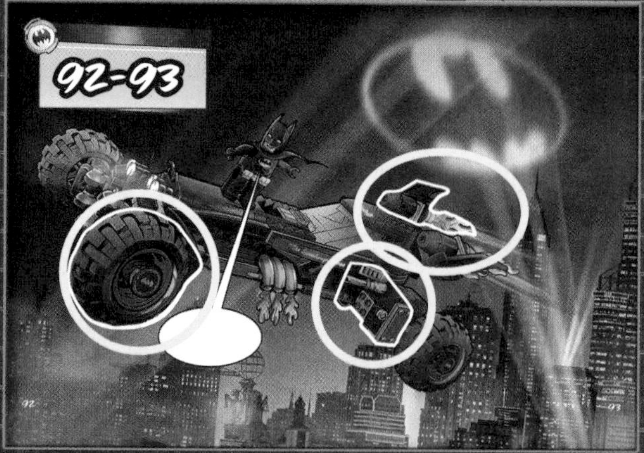
92-93

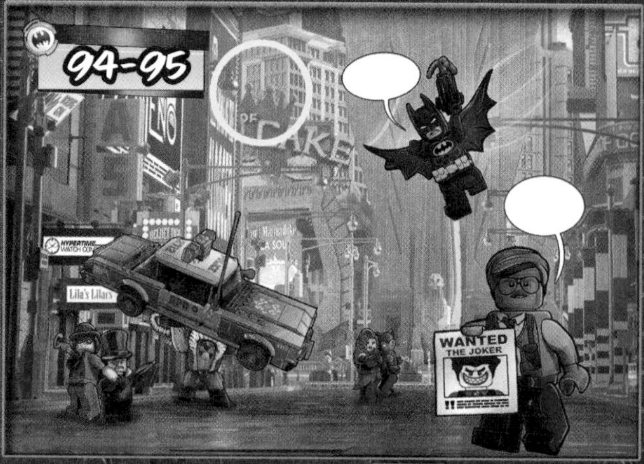
94-95
Lila's Lilacs
WANTED
THE JOKER

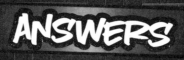